The
Kinfolk

By Eliza Maxwell

Carter Literary Press
547 William D Fitch Pkwy
Suite 105
College Station, TX 77845

Printed in the United States of America

Second Edition: March 2017
10 9 8 7 6 5 4 3 2 1

ASIN: B01GNSVWTU
ISBN-13: 978-1520890043

DEDICATION

For my own kinfolk and the endless supply of front porches, sweet tea, and encouragement. I write fiction because I come from a family full of bullshitters—except for my brother. His stories are all true.

CONTENTS

ACKNOWLEDGMENTS

To my kids, bless you both. Without you this book would never have been written, because if I could get anyone to listen to me at home I wouldn't feel compelled to write stories for strangers.

To the strangers reading this, thank you, from the bottom of my heart. Get in touch, we'll be friends.

PART I

LONG BROKEN AND GONE

Butt-up to the moment the man in the white linen suit sat down at her bar Mimosa Mabry'd been having a fine day.

"Mo, my dearest lovely, you're almost smiling."

Doc's words weren't runny yet, only Scottish, so she pulled a fresh pint from the tap and gently slid it over to him.

"What's it to you? I can't be in a good mood?"

He took a long sniff of the beer before downing half in a few gulps.

"Oh, aye, you can. Just wondering what's got you so cheery. You find a nice big bag of kittens to gnaw on for yer breakfast?"

"You've got jokes. That's cute."

"Cute enough for a date?" He wriggled a bushy grey eyebrow at her.

"What are you gonna do, old man, when I decide to say yes, one of these days?"

He clutched his chest.

"I don't know if me old ticker could take it, love. But I'd die a happy man."

Her laugh made a rare appearance. It was strong and earthy. Sexual, almost, and surprising. In a bar where several nearly naked women danced, heads lifted and tilted her way. Wolves trying to catch a scent that had already passed them by; each slightly more discontent than before, they went back to their drinks.

The neon-pink sign out front read Lingerie Lounge. It sported a disembodied leg in a fishnet and high heel. Locals referred to the place, more fittingly, as Dirty Knickers, or just plain Nick's. The name clung so tightly that the owner, a fat man who smelled like cheese, had answered to the name Big Nick for so long that no one but his mother remembered, or cared, that his real name was Bruce.

Mo's laugh brought Nick wandering out of his office. He found his way to the bar where he stood awkwardly with his hands in his pockets. Nick always kept his hands in his pockets around Mo. He did now, anyway.

"I don't suppose you paid for that?" he asked, nodding to the pint in front of Doc.

"His tab is covered," Mo said, her face hard and her laughter gone like it'd never been.

"Mooching off the girls again, Doc?"

"Payment in kind for services rendered." Doc took another gulp while Nick looked impotently on. This was nothing new. Complaining would do him no good at all. Mo and the girls paid the old drunk's tab daily, which never amounted to much anyway. But feigned camaraderie was better than none at all. Nick persisted.

Mo might have felt some sympathy, if she'd been the type. Big Nick wasn't a bad man, she knew. But that didn't make him a good one.

As for Doc, he'd twice chased off grabbers looking to take more from the girls than was offered. His wild-eyed, nothing-to-lose, banshee yell did the job perfectly well, but he kept a broken golf club hooked in his belt, just in case.

Mo herself had never needed his help. She wasn't that type either.

She'd heard the Scotsman's tale about how he'd ended up in Texas many times. Each time the story changed, but two things remained the same. It always involved a woman, and he was always full of it.

But Mo liked him. An uncommon thing.

When the door opened the man in white entered, blinking away the Texas sun. The mostly useless bouncer on the door stopped him and he fumbled in his wallet for the twelve-dollar cover. He seemed happy enough to hand it over.

It wasn't his silver hair and well-trimmed beard or his cream linen suit that marked him out of his element—the place attracted all kinds. It was the way he looked around, his eyes a bit wide, like a preteen who'd never seen real live breasts before.

This man was a long way from home.

When he pulled up a barstool he had an unassuming air about him, but Mo wasn't fooled.

She moved down the bar toward him.

"What do you want?" she asked without preamble.

"Long Island Iced Tea," he said, with a question in his voice, as if he needed her permission.

"Don't mess around with me. What do you want?"

A wounded look crossed his face. It may have been genuine, but she didn't care.

"Could I get a drink, Mimosa? Please," he added quietly.

"Fine," she said.

Her hands moved behind the bar, splashing liquor into a glass, her haste giving away the agitation that her face was trying to hide. She set the glass in front of him.

"You drink your drink. And then I want you gone."

"Don't you even want to hear—"

"No. I don't."

Mo grabbed a clean rag and turned her back, wiping down glassware and trying her damnedest to ignore the man.

"It's Rosalind."

Mo's hands went still but only for a moment.

"Is she dead?"

"She's… unwell."

Mo turned back to the man, one raised eyebrow the only sign she cared slightly more than not at all.

"She's sick?" Mo asked.

"You could say that," he said, sipping his drink.

Mo squinted at the man she hadn't seen in at least a decade, wondering, against her better judgement, about all he wasn't saying.

"So what?"

"So what?" He repeated. "Is that all you have to say, Mimosa?"

She crossed her arms and stared at him, unmoving.

"Can I get another beer down here?" called Doc from the other end of the bar.

"Yeah, Doc, you got it." She stared at the man for another moment, giving him one last chance to say more, then dismissed him.

"That guy bothering you?" Doc asked loudly.

For a moment, Mo considered saying yes just to see Doc in action, but she didn't want him fussing. He had a bad hip and blood pressure problems.

"No, Doc. He's leaving," she said, although the man in question didn't seem ready to take the hint.

Instead, he sipped his drink and called down the bar, "Roz wants you to come home, Mo."

For the first time since Hayes Ivey walked through the door, Mo was truly shocked. Her mouth hung open as she turned to the man in disbelief.

"Home?" she asked, disbelieving. "To Red Poppy?"

She shook her head. "You can't be serious."

"Oh, she's serious all right," Hayes said.

"But… what on God's green earth would make her think I'd be willing—" She stopped herself, shaking her head.

Hayes looked like he was searching for words, ready to plead a case.

"You know what," she said, holding up a hand to cut off

whatever he was about to say. "Never mind. It doesn't matter."

Hayes opened his mouth to speak again, but she preempted him.

"No. I don't care. I don't care what you're going to say. I don't care what Roz wants. I don't care. The answer is no."

She waited until he closed his mouth, making sure he'd heard what she'd said.

"Now I want you to leave."

"Mimosa—"

She turned her back on him, the bar rag twisting in her hands.

Mo heard him sigh.

"She told me you'd be this way, but I didn't realize... I thought..." Hayes was mumbling to himself, but Mo kept her back turned, willing him to go away before she lost her grip.

"Roz said you wouldn't come. She knew. So she told me what to say. She said..." Hayes sighed again.

"She said, come home and she'd tell you the truth about Lucy," he said in a rush.

With her back still to him, Hayes didn't see Mo's face change. Didn't see the bomb drop behind her eyes. He had no idea what those words did to her.

"Lucy's dead," she whispered.

"Is she?" Hayes said. "Or is that the only way you'd let her go?"

"Get out." Her voice was hoarse, raw.

Hayes stood, retrieving his hat. He spoke quietly, but she still heard him say, "You've changed, Mimosa Mabry. You're harder than you used to be."

"You have no idea," she mumbled to herself.

When she finally turned around, he was gone. He'd left behind a twenty-dollar bill and a business card.

T. Hayes Ivey
Attorney at Law

She flipped it over. He'd written on the back, EconoLodge - Room 223. Her eyes were hot. She was shocked to realize how close to tears she was. Ripping the card in half and tossing the pieces into the trash, she slid the twenty over to Doc.

No, she thought, swiping at the damning wetness around her eyes. *No tears. Not for Hayes Ivey. And certainly not for Roz.*

The voice on the phone sounded anything but sick.

"Is she coming?"

Hayes sighed. "She despises you, Rosalind."

"But is she coming?"

Hayes shook his head. "What have you done to that girl, Roz?"

"Nothing," she said. "Everything. Oh, shut up Hayes. You know exactly what I've done."

"I thought she might've forgiven you by now."

The laughter on the other end of the line was harsh.

"Then you're a fool."

"That's been established."

"You don't know her. She's never gonna forgive me, so it's a good thing that's not what I'm after."

"Rosalind, being your friend is one of the hardest thing I've ever done."

"So don't be," she said. "I don't need friends. But I do need that girl home. Find a way Hayes."

The line went dead.

Her friend Georgia had given Mo a ride to her apartment. She'd offered to stay, but Mo had said she was fine and sent Georgia home to wash off the glitter body spray and the stench of cigarette smoke that a shift stripping at Nick's leaves behind. Alone now, Mo was surprised to find she wished her friend hadn't listened.

The buzz she'd nurtured with shots of tequila throughout the night to hold the emotions at bay had worn off. It was too quiet, with only the ceiling fan clicking, and she found the liquor had weakened her walls.

The apartment looked different.

In a style she called utilitarian and Georgia called depressing, there was no comfort to be found in the blank walls and secondhand furniture. That had never bothered her before. But now, the place felt... empty. She wandered around, seeing it with new eyes.

She didn't even have a cat.

Mo wasn't given to introspection. She found she didn't care for it much. A life led at an arm's length from most of the human race had granted her a sense of peace once.

But that was gone.

The past seeped in through the cracks and pooled at her feet.

Oddly, it wasn't memories of Roz she found herself surrounded by but memories of her mother, Della.

Even before their boho days together, there'd been a sense of contentment. Her earliest memories were vague impressions of laughter, sunshine. Of her mother's arms. Of safety at Red Poppy Ridge. She never knew what had happened between her mother and Roz, but those days were long broken and gone.

The same as she felt now. Hayes' words had pried her open, and the life she'd been leading had escaped. Mo knew the futility of trying to chase smoke. It wasn't coming back.

She found herself wishing she had a memento of Lucy, something physical to hold and touch. But all she had left was a hole. The burden had been heavy enough. Now, it was impossible.

Roz was lying. Of that much, she was certain. It was a trick, a play to get her to do the woman's bidding. And yet...

After a lifetime spent never looking back, Mo found she

couldn't imagine going forward. Not without knowing. Not if she wanted to keep her sanity intact.

To an observer, she'd have appeared calm. They wouldn't see the cornered desperation barely contained below the surface. But it was there all the same.

She picked up her phone and looked up the number for the EconoLodge.

WAVERLY PUBLIC LIBRARY

"I still can't believe that loser hit you," Mo said, glancing across the front seat of the old jeep at Georgia.

"Honestly, neither can I," Georgia said, lifting her sunglasses to inspect her black eye in the mirror on the back of the visor. The bruise was fresh, and the make-up she'd applied did little to mask it. She shook her head at her reflection.

"I can't tell you how many times I saw my mom like this. I swore to myself that it'd never be me." She clenched her jaw and snapped the visor back against the roof of the car. "Thanks for letting me tag along. It's better that Jack won't be able to find me for the moment."

"I'm glad to have the company," Mo said. Georgia was one of the few she could call a friend. She'd been tempted to find Jack O'Shea and kick his teeth in when she'd seen the black eye, but Georgia assured her it was unnecessary.

"I rearranged his testicles for him before I packed my bags," she'd said.

Mo was more grateful than she liked to admit that she wouldn't be making this trip alone.

"Did Nick give you a hard time about the time off?" Georgia asked.

"He did look kind of put upon, but why should he? I've worked there three years without a vacation, and Toby's trained. The place will be fine. What about you?"

"He just sighed and looked like I'd kicked his dog."

"You're not going to go back to him, are you?"

Georgia glanced over at her at the sudden change of subject.

"Jack? Please. I'm not afraid to be alone. Besides, I have you and this mysterious road trip to keep me occupied." She sent her friend a rueful smile, ready to talk about something else.

"When are you gonna tell me what this is all about, anyway?"

"It's not mysterious. Just family," Mo said, avoiding the specifics.

"Hmm. I've never heard you talk about your family."

"We're not exactly close."

"So I gathered. What are they like?"

Uncomfortable, Mo looked like she wasn't going to answer. Finally, though, she said, "I don't know. Typical, I guess. Liars, thieves and fools. Why do you want to know?"

"Because you're my friend, you jerk. You know all about my family's dysfunctional corner of the world, but for all you've never said, you may as well have been sprung fully-formed from the depths of the sea. Or behind the bar at Nick's."

"It's not that interesting, trust me."

"We have hours. Bore me. Start with the thieves and go from there."

Mo gave in. "That would be my uncle, Arlo Vaughn."

"What'd he steal?"

"Probably nothing. My aunt, Roz, always acted like those stories were just so much hot air, something that Arlo spread around to make a reputation for himself."

Georgia raised an eyebrow, prompting Mo to go on.

"Rumor has it, Arlo was a bank robber. Back in the day."

Georgia's mouth dropped open.

"But like I said, that place is so full of lies they meet up and breed little baby lies. And I've only met Arlo a few times anyway. He and my aunt split a long time ago."

"And that's where we're going? Your aunt's house?"

Mo nodded. "Red Poppy Ridge. I lived there when I was

a teenager."

"Your family home has a name? Is this like some old Southern plantation with a tragic history of abuse and slavery? Ghosts and batty old women locked in the attic?"

"Not quite," Mo said, grinning at Georgia's disappointment.

"I suppose it could look a little *plantationish*," she said, to placate her friend. "If it weren't red."

"Red?" Georgia asked.

Mo nodded. "It's a long story."

"What, you have somewhere else to be?"

"You really want to hear this?"

"Uh, yeah. I do. Get on with it."

"Okay, fine. So, the first owner, the guy who built the place, was a ferryman. The house is on a river, the Neches. Under normal circumstances, being a ferryman doesn't pay terribly well, but he was also the gatekeeper for the local version of the red-light district."

"Prostitution? You're kidding, right?"

"Nope. There's a row of cabins there, just upriver, that can only be accessed by water. That's where he'd take you if you were looking for a good time. For a price, of course."

"You're serious?"

"Oh yeah. He was raking it in hand over fist. He built the cabins in the first place, on a worthless piece of land he'd inherited from his own dad. People wondered what he was thinking, building on a piece of rock that could only be reached from the river, but he knew what he was doing. He brought in the girls, charged them rent, then charged the customers his taxi fee. To top it off, he ran a high stakes poker game out of one of the cabins. Apparently, he didn't gamble himself. Devout Baptist." The corner of Mo's mouth lifted. "But he had no problem taking a cut off the top."

"And this guy was related to you how?"

"Grandfather, a few greats back."

"So what you're telling me is your great, great grandfather

ran a backwater bordello and illegal gambling house. And you don't think that's interesting?"

"Believe me, when you're forced to live in that house, the novelty wears thin."

"So why's the house red?"

"Somewhere along the way, Granddad got himself a prissy wife. Probably bought her at the church bake sale. That's who he built the house for. But Mrs. Bordello liked to put on airs, so the story goes. So he had the house painted red. To remind her that the money she liked to throw around was earned off of women on their backs."

"So he was a jerk, too."

"Pretty much. Tends to run in the family."

"All of them?"

"No. My Uncle Calvin, Roz's brother, he's all right. Lives in what used to be a guest house. You'll like him. And there's Phillip, my cousin, if he's still around. Phillip... well, let's just say that being Roz's kid comes with its own set of challenges. But Phillip helped keep me sane. After things got bad. Or helped me go crazy, depending on who you ask."

"And your aunt?"

Mo's face grew hard.

"Aunt Rosalind. Can't forget her." She was silent for a beat.

"Did I mention the liars? That'd be Roz."

Mo didn't say any more. Georgia could see she'd struck a nerve and laid off the questions for the rest of the drive.

✳

It took five hours to reach their destination. Mo couldn't help but feel it should've taken longer. That somehow, it should be more difficult to reach a place she'd spent a decade putting behind her. Burning lakes of fire and desert wastelands belching sulfur to cross. Something.

But it was dishearteningly easy for the wheels on the jeep to take them out of the central Texas hill country, right into the shadows of the pine belt. One minute it was bluebonnets along the roadside. The next, they were being swallowed by towering conifers.

East Texas. A land unto itself. With geography that was more Louisiana than Texas and a pervasive attitude that was almost tribal, Mo had shaken the mud of this place off her boots and never looked back.

They passed a sign that read Justus, Texas Pop. 867.

It had bullet holes in it.

Passing through the middle of town, they stopped at the two red lights. Mo tried to keep her eyes forward, focused on the horse trailer on the road in front of them, but she couldn't help notice the old storefronts with open signs. They were the same. All the same, hawking their questionable antiques and auto parts. She could picture the proprietors, mummified and propped up behind the counters. She wondered why they didn't just close them down.

In spite of her growing unease, the jeep carried them forward and they passed through town, coming eventually to the turnoff for the gravel road that would lead her to her aunt.

She stopped at the entrance, her heart beating in her chest.

Georgia looked at her with concern as she gripped the wheel.

"We can go back, you know. Just turn around and drive away. You don't have to do this if you don't want to."

Mo longed to do just that. But she thought of Lucy. Of the paralyzing impossibility of living with the unanswered questions Hayes Ivey had dropped in her lap.

"No. It's too late for that."

She put the jeep in drive and headed up the road.

The twin gravel tracks wound around, through the trees. If you knew when and where to look, you could catch a glimpse of the river through the gaps, but Mo was too distracted to point it out. The road broke through the trees which gave way to a clearing, and there it stood in the distance, resting along a bend in the river.

Red Poppy Ridge.

The place was showing its age. Mo could see where the roof needed mending. The porch sagged to the right. The paint, so vibrant when her aunt had it updated every few years, was faded to the color of an old blood stain. The house was an aging prostitute, sunning herself by the riverbank, waiting for midnight when her cracks and crags could hide behind the darkness.

The jeep pulled them closer, gravel crunching under the tires.

And like an apparition, born from her thoughts and made visible, there was a girl.

Mo blinked. But she was still there, standing on the porch under the sagging roof.

Mo didn't remember putting the jeep in park, or stepping out into the sun. She made no conscious decision to walk slowly up to the house, pulled forward on legs that moved of their own volition, her own heart's bass rhythm pounding in her ears. As Mo took the porch steps one by one, she was afraid the girl would flicker and vanish before her eyes.

And yet, when she knelt in front of her, the girl remained. Her hair was dark and long and glossy. Although she didn't speak, there was a placid serenity that filled the girl's brown eyes.

Mo could hardly recall what Red Beechum's face looked like. He was a character who'd exited her stage a long time ago. Though he'd had a vital role, it was a bit part, at best. She struggled now to recall his features.

Those could be his eyes. Was she imagining a familiar tilt to the chin?

"Lucy?" she whispered, reaching slowly upward to stroke the girl's hair.

Everything. Everything hinged on the girl's words. Mo waited with her breath in her throat, willing the girl to say the words.

But no words came.

When the dark haired girl slowly shook her head, Mo

wondered that her limbs could move at all. How was she supposed to stand when her body was filled with stones?

But she did stand.

"Mo?" Georgia called, from miles, years away. It pulled her back from the precipice she'd been teetering on. She found grief eagerly waiting for her.

"Stay here," Mo said to her friend. Then she went to find her aunt.

Throwing the front door open, Mo barely registered the state of the house, a shrine Rosalind kept to a moldering past dead and gone. Her aunt's tendency to hoard had worsened through the years, but Mo wasn't interested in Roz's housekeeping at the moment.

"Roz," she called, her voice strident and jarring in the dust particles and accumulated junk.

There was no reply.

Mo forced herself to move deeper into the aging mausoleum, propelled to find the woman who'd brought her here. A hint of voices drew her down the hallway to the bedroom of her aunt.

"Who is that girl?" she demanded at the open door.

"And hello to you too," said the woman propped up in the bed. "I see your manners haven't improved."

"Don't play games with me, Roz. I'm not in the mood."

The woman smiled, but it was joyless.

"That makes two of us then, child."

The room could almost have been the same as it'd always been. Except for the presence of the hospital style bed her aunt lay upon. That and the grim faced woman who was seated in a chair along the wall.

The woman's name was Iona. The last time Mo had seen her she'd been pushing a needle into Mo's arm.

She found that the hatred she had for these women hadn't mellowed with time but felt as fresh as a rotting cadaver.

"Who is that girl?" she demanded again, louder this time.

"There's no need to raise your voice, Mimosa," Roz said.

She forced herself to take the time to form a coherent

thought before she spoke.

In a whisper this time, Mo said, "Rosalind, if you don't answer me, you won't have to worry about me raising my voice again."

Mo took a threatening step forward.

"Because if I don't get an answer, I will burn this house down around your ears. Now. I will ask you one last time. Who. Is. That. Girl?"

"Threats are unnecessary, Mimosa Jane," Roz said, quietly but unbowed. "Her name is Emma. You might remember her mother. I believe she's about your age. Abigail Fontaine."

And with those words, Mo's rage crumbled into the dust of a very old and familiar pain. All fight gone from her, Mo took a deep breath.

"What do you want from me, Roz?"

Her aunt turned her head and glanced at Iona. Without a word passing between them, the woman raised her ponderous frame and lifted a glass with a straw in it to Roz's lips.

Against her better judgement, Mo wondered what ailed her aunt, that she couldn't even raise her own glass. The hands lying by her side seemed fine. But Mo couldn't gather enough concern to ask.

"I want you to come home."

Mo gave a harsh bark of laughter. "I'm here, aren't I? But don't lie to yourself Roz. This has never been my home."

"Be that as it may," the older woman said. "You misunderstand me."

"Finally, we agree on something. I've never understood you."

Mo could see she was getting under the other woman's skin. She took a small satisfaction in it.

"Mimosa, I did not bring you here for a visit. I expect you to stay."

Any satisfaction fled, replaced by shock. She stared at Roz, but her aunt's expression gave away nothing but an iron determination that Mo remembered well.

"You're serious."

"Oh yes."

Emotions competed inside Mo. Cold logic won out.

"You're not fool enough to believe I'd stay here based on tricks and games."

"No," Roz agreed.

"Then why? What could you possibly say that would keep me here in this place I swore I'd never come back to? That girl? That's not Lucy. Lucy's dead."

Mo longed for her aunt to admit the truth, severing the final tie that Roz and Hayes had woven out of lies and deceit. The tie that had pulled her here and held her still.

"No. That's not Lucy."

But she said nothing more.

"Then why should I do anything for you at all?"

"Because, Mimosa. There's more to know."

"There's nothing more! There are no words to say that can construct a daughter out of ash."

"One month. Stay here for one month, as I ask. Then you can decide for yourself whether those words matter. In one month, you'll have earned those words."

"You're insane," Mo said, shaking her head at the fantastical request.

"One month and you can pass judgements on the state of my sanity all you like."

"No."

The two women, united by blood, but opposed by their very different agendas locked eyes in a battle of wills both were destined to lose.

"Then go," Roz said. "The choice is yours."

Without another word, Mo turned and fled the room. Fled from the terrible possibilities she'd been presented. She had to stop herself from breaking into a run as she made her way down the hallway and back out the front door. She desperately needed to breathe. Even the thick, humid heat was an improvement over the smell of decay and deceit that permeated the house.

She put her hands on her knees and breathed in the scents of pine and river in great, gasping bites.

But the panic didn't lessen.

The girl, the dark haired child born from another woman's womb, was gone. Mo could be grateful for that.

She headed straight to her jeep, taking inordinate comfort in the physical sign that the last ten years had actually happened. That this wasn't some fevered dream she'd awoken from to find herself trapped in this place once again.

Behind the wheel, she fumbled for the keys, dropping them in the floorboard.

"Damn, damn, damn," she cursed as she felt around for them, grasping them in her hand like a lifeline, as an additional thought broke through.

Georgia.

"Damn." Mo glanced around, but her friend wasn't in sight. Unable to bring herself to step foot out of the jeep again, she laid into the horn, willing the other woman to materialize.

When no one came, she leaned her head against the steering wheel.

Breathe, she told herself. Just breathe.

Mo didn't know how long she stayed that way. Her sense of time passing around her was skewed by the panic she was fighting against.

Eventually, there came a knock on her window.

Tap, tap, tap, it said.

She was hoping for Georgia. Once she was able to force her head away from the wheel and look up, it was Calvin she found.

With a sigh, she opened the door of the jeep and got out to greet her uncle.

"How've you been, Mo?" Calvin asked.

"I've had better days."

The two of them had walked down by the river.

The river.

If there was anything Mo had missed about this place, it was this. There was a peace to be found here. A peace she'd never known anywhere else.

The water rolled by, unfazed by the goings on around it. And why should it be? The river endured it all.

"I know this is hard for you, but I can't say I'm sorry to see you again," Calvin said.

She could say something about never planning to come back here, but she was tired of hearing herself. Calvin knew that already. And it sounded like whining, even inside her own head.

"What's wrong with her?" she asked instead.

"I assume you mean physically."

That got a small smile.

"Yeah."

"Good. Because I can't even begin to explain the workings of my sister's mind."

"Join the club."

Calvin took a seat next to her on the riverbank where the pine needles made a prickly layer over the damp soil. He fished a small wooden box from his pocket and set his able hands to work.

He still rolled the tightest joint Mo had ever seen.

After he took the first drag, he offered it to Mo, but she declined.

Shrugging, he took a moment for the marijuana to settle upon his shoulders like a fuzzy blanket.

She waited.

"Roz is paralyzed," Calvin said, blowing out smoke. "From the neck down."

Whatever she'd thought he might say, that wasn't it.

But after the initial shock gave way, Mo remembered her aunt's hands, lying on the quilt that covered her from the waist down. The seemingly uninjured hands that couldn't lift her own glass. She remembered the stillness of the woman, so unlike the Roz she'd known, who'd always strode through life with an entitled grace.

"How?" Mo asked.

"She was attacked. Left for dead. I found her myself, the next day."

Calvin's gaze stayed on the opposite shoreline, but she could hear unspoken things lurking behind his matter of fact words.

"Oh my God."

"Burglars probably, according to the police. There were some things taken." Calvin shook his head. "Although how she can tell in that mess is anyone's guess."

"Did they catch them?" Mo asked.

"No. She says she doesn't remember anything. She took a blow to the head. The doctors said her memory of it might come back. Or it might not."

He took another drag off his joint.

"They hit her hard enough to break her neck. It damaged her spinal cord beyond repair."

Mo didn't know what to say. She couldn't pretend she felt any differently toward Rosalind than she did. But sweet Jesus.

"The sheriff's department, they want to talk to Phillip," Calvin went on.

"Phillip? Surely they don't think he did this. To his own mother?"

"I let slip I'd seen him that day, heading over to the big house. It was right after; the cops were asking me questions. I wasn't really thinking of him as a suspect, just that he might have seen something, heard something. I don't know."

Calvin shook his head.

"But he's up and disappeared. No one's seen him since then."

"You think he did this? Phillip?"

"I'm not saying that. Though Lord knows there's no love lost between those two. So far as I know, the cops just want to talk to him is all."

Calvin took another drag.

"But hiding out this way. That makes him look like he has something to hide. The dumb shit."

Mo shook her head. "I can't believe Phillip would do something like this."

Her uncle gave her a sad little smile.

"You've been gone a long time, Mo."

So she had. Her face must have given away her troubled thoughts.

"It's good to have you back, though."

She shook her head at that. "I'm not back. Not really."

"No?"

"No."

He let that slide. She was glad for it.

"I still don't understand. That hatchet-faced friend of hers is a nurse. Supposedly. It's not like she needs me to empty bedpans. What does she want with me, Cal?"

Her uncle looked over in surprise.

"She didn't tell you?"

Mo merely raised an eyebrow.

"No. What am I saying. Of course she didn't."

Calvin sighed.

"You met Emma."

"The dark haired girl? Yeah. What about her?"

"She's the reason you're here. One of the reasons, at least."

"Cal, somebody'd better start explaining to me what the hell is going on."

Calvin started to speak, then thought better of it. He rose and offered her a hand up.

"I think we'd better call Hayes."

"Have you seen Georgia?" Mo asked.

"The blonde that looks like Bridget Bardot?"

"That'd be her."

"She's at my place with Emma. Do you want to go get her? Moral support?"

Mo shook her head.

"I'm fine. As long as you didn't lock her in a tower somewhere."

"Tempting. If only I had a tower." He appeared to consider it. "I should really build a tower."

Mo had forgotten the ease of her uncle. Without realizing it, he'd managed to calm her nerves while they waited, at least a little, just by being who he was.

Although she still wouldn't step foot back inside the house.

When Hayes arrived, he joined them, taking a seat in one of the moldy wicker chairs that graced the moldy front porch. Calvin had brought out some iced tea from the house.

Mo's thoughts strayed unwillingly to Roz, unmoving in her bed. More than just a few walls separated them.

Her aunt was the one trapped now, burdened with a body that refused to obey.

Mo could find no pleasure in the thought.

Hayes dug a handkerchief out of his pocket and wiped the sweat from his brow. The fact that he carried a handkerchief spoke volumes about the man.

"Tell her about Emma," Calvin said.

Hayes nodded. "Of course."

But he seemed to lose his words as he fiddled with his sweaty handkerchief.

"Well," Mo prodded. What little patience she had, she was hanging onto by a very frayed thread.

"Of course," he said again, clearing his throat.

"Emma's mother, Abigail Fontaine—Do you remember her?"

Mo nodded. Abby Fontaine was difficult to forget.

"She was beautiful."

Hayes nodded. "She still is. She's also batshit crazy."

Mo's forehead creased in confusion. "Crazy? I

remember she was religious. Kind of quiet. But crazy?"

"Oh yes," Hayes said.

Mo glanced at Calvin, who nodded in agreement. "As a loon," he added.

Hayes went on. "Abby found herself a husband right out of high school. A girl that looks like that doesn't stay single for long if she doesn't want to. And some roughneck Lothario from over Cordelia way swept her off her feet. Emma was born within the year."

Mo wondered what this had to do with her aunt, or with her, but she held her tongue.

"Nobody knows if Abby really started hearing voices, or if she just said that to stop her husband from beating on her. I suppose it doesn't matter much. The end result was the same.

"She said God was telling her things. Being a God fearing man himself, well... I don't know if he believed her or not, but either way he didn't hit her again. But he found he couldn't live with that brand of extra-strength religion either, so he brought her back to Justus and dropped her off where he'd picked her up. Her and the baby, both."

"Let me guess," Mo said. "He was never seen or heard from again."

Hayes nodded. "Except for the divorce papers that showed up a few years later."

He continued. "They lived with Abby's mother for a few years, but when Mary passed, there was no family left. Her father, Bernon, had eaten his gun years ago. After that, the voices pretty much took over."

"Has she seen a doctor? There are medications..."

Hayes nodded his head. "There are. And when she takes them, she improves. But with no one around except a little girl, who's gonna make sure she stays on them? Besides, Abby doesn't like it when the voices go away. Says it makes her feel like she's done something wrong."

A picture rose in Mo's mind of Emma's placid blue eyes. She felt something she wasn't looking to feel.

"Where does Roz come into this?"

"After the child was found on the front steps of the Methodist church with a sign around her neck that proclaimed her in need of the Lord's cleansing, Roz chose to step in."

"She has a tendency to do that," Mo said.

"The child's skin had been scrubbed nearly raw. And there was a dead bird stapled to the note," Hayes said sharply.

Tempering her judgement, Mo nodded.

"Children's Protective Services had been by the house before, but the truth is, CPS doesn't like to take kids from their parents. Not without undeniable cause. The foster system... let's just say the agents know that these kids are often better off where they're at, no matter how batshit their mother is."

"Roz didn't agree, I take it."

"I don't know what she said to Abigail. All I know is, she went over there. When she came back, Emma came with her."

Mo sat back in her chair. Understanding had finally dawned.

"She wants me here to take care of the kid."

Hayes looked uncomfortable, but he didn't deny it.

"Roz has no legal standing in this, you see. There's been no paperwork filed. No guardianship or custody. Just a child living here, with what we can only assume is her mother's consent."

Mo didn't need to ask why her aunt had bypassed official channels. Rosalind had always done things that way. She had a blazing disregard for society's expectations.

Mo was silent. The two men waited for her to speak.

"Look. It's not that I'm unmoved. I'm not a monster—"

"There are two more," Calvin said, cutting off what she was about to say.

"Two more what?" Mo asked.

"Two more kids. Tate's eleven. And Sadie's only six."

Mo stared at her uncle, speechless.

"Suffice it to say," Hayes went on, "their situations, though different from Emma's in detail, have also brought them here."

"Three?" Mo said in awe. "She expects me to stay here and play Mary Poppins to three orphaned kids?"

"Technically speaking, none of them are orphans," Hayes hastened to say.

"Technically speaking? Technically speaking?" Her voice was rising.

"I came here because Roz, and you," she said, pointing a finger at Hayes, "dangled some fabricated story about the only thing that's ever mattered to me. She used me, and you helped her do it!"

"Mimosa—"

"Don't Mimosa me!" she said. "I came back here on the false possibility of some sort of truth about Lucy, not to take care of three unfortunates!"

"Hey, kid, you were one of those unfortunates once," Calvin said.

"I was not." Mo spit out the words. "I never wanted to be here. Don't fool yourself into believing that Rosalind Mabry ever did me any favors."

Calvin shut his mouth at that.

"You take them then," she went on. "If you're so concerned. I don't see you stepping up to the plate, buddy."

Her uncle shook his head.

"CPS turns a blind eye to the kids living with Roz. But me? A single, middle-aged man of questionable reputation and income? No. They'd snatch them out of here and put them back with their parents, or worse, in foster care, faster than you can hang a dead bird around a kid's neck."

Mo rose, trying to shake off the image and walked to the edge of the porch.

Her jeep was right there. It was so close. Ready and able to take her out of here, away from this pit of memories and pain.

"I don't have the answers you're looking for. About Lucy," Hayes said from behind her. She was glad he couldn't see her face.

"Only Roz can answer those questions."

He almost sounded kind.

But Calvin didn't bother being kind when he added, "And Roz isn't talking. Not unless you do what she wants."

Mo remembered this feeling all too well. The helplessness of being steered against her will by the desires of her inscrutable aunt.

"Stay," Calvin said. "Stay for these kids. Stay to find out your truth."

She gave a harsh laugh.

"There's no truth here," she said. "There never was."

"I'll stay," Mo said.

Her aunt showed no reaction to the news.

"I won't promise for how long."

"One month," Roz said. Mo fought off the urge to scream.

"One month and I'll give you what you want."

"What I want? That's good, Roz. As if that's in your power to give."

Her niece's disregard rolled off of the woman without making a perceptible mark. That was nothing new. Losing the use of her body had only made her more implacable.

"You've trapped me here. Again."

"If that's the way you see it, then so be it."

Mo turned and left. She needed to find her friend.

Calvin's place may have shared the property with his sister's, but that's where the similarities ended. The guest house was clean, first of all. The interior was tidy in a minimalist way that allowed the boldness of the few furnishings and paintings on the walls to stand out.

But the oversized windows along three walls were the stars

of the show. Natural light poured into the space. There were no chintzy curtains or blinds to block the view of the woods and the river beyond.

It was breathtaking.

That was where she found Georgia, playing video games with a skinny, scruffy boy with mouse brown hair. Emma was there also, curled into the corner of an overstuffed chair with a book. And there was another girl as well, a smaller one. Mo struggled to recall her name. Susie? Sophie?

The child was lying on the floor with papers and crayons strewn about her like casualties of a war. The body count was high. Her legs scissored in the air behind her while she concentrated on her artwork.

Emma noticed Mo first, looking up and laying the book in her hand against her chest. The others were caught up in what they were doing.

"Go, go, go, go, go," the boy urged, leaning hard to the right, both of his thumbs working the buttons of the game controller like a madman. Georgia was smiling, but she was working over the other controller with just as much determination when a sudden explosion came from the big screen. Georgia dropped her controller and threw up her hands, yelling in victory, while the boy moaned, planting himself face first into the couch cushions.

"Yes! Still the undisputed champ!"

There were some muffled words trying to escape the cushions, but they didn't make it.

"What'd I tell you? Girl or not, I have three brothers and mad skills. That'll teach you to underestimate a girl, my friend."

Lifting his head a bit, the boy asked, "Rematch?"

"Potty break," Georgia said. She rose, ruffling the boy's already ruffled head as it dropped back down on the couch in defeat.

Mo caught her eye when she stood and gestured with her head in what she hoped was a *We need to talk* sort of way. Apparently she needed some practice.

"Mo, come meet my new friends," Georgia said, not catching the head gesture at all.

The little blonde girl on the floor turned toward them and the boy's mousy head rose up over the back of the couch. Emma hadn't taken her eyes off of Mo since she'd walked in the door.

Unbidden, Mo thought of the meerkats at the Waco zoo.

Some funny guy had decided to locate their enclosure right next door to the lion enclosure. Their daily lives were punctuated by the bellowing roar of a predator they could neither see nor control. The little creatures went about their day, but the sounds and scents of danger were always there, just around the corner, and they never forgot it.

"Who are you?" the little one asked.

"Um. My name is Mo. I'm Roz's niece."

Two of the three faces showed their suspicions clearly. The third probably felt it too, Mo thought. She was just better at hiding it.

"I've been here almost two years. I've never heard of you," the boy said.

"Guess you don't know everything, then," Mo snapped. The boy's face hardened. Mo was disgusted with herself. That irritated her more.

"Are you always in a bad mood?" the little girl on the floor asked.

"Lately, yes."

Her blonde head tilted a bit to one side.

"Are you nice when you're not?"

An honest question.

"Not very," Mo said, albeit in a gentler tone.

The little girl nodded, accepting the honest reply.

"This is Sadie, Tate and Emma," Georgia said, gesturing to the kids in turn.

"I'm sorry if I frightened you earlier," Mo said to Emma, but the girl just stared back at her.

"She doesn't talk," Tate said, glaring at Mo.

"Not at all?" she asked him.

He shook his head.

"Guess you don't know everything either." He rose from the couch. "Come on, let's get out of here," he said to the others.

Emma clutched her battered paperback to her chest and followed Tate as he brushed past the two women on his way to the front door. Georgia gave them both a smile as they passed.

Sadie put her crayons away, then moved to follow.

"Don't mind him," she said to Mo. "Roz says he's always got a bug up his butt about something. Must be itchy." Then she was gone too.

"Wait for me," they heard her call as the door shut behind her.

"I am continually amazed at your ability to win friends and influence people, Mo," Georgia said with a smile.

"That's me. Miss Congeniality."

"So what's the story here?"

Mo sighed.

"I need a drink."

They stole two beers from Cal's well-stocked bachelor's fridge and Mo filled her in on the highlights.

Once the initial shock and disbelief received the appropriate recognition, Georgia gave a low whistle and leaned back against the bar stool in Calvin's kitchen.

"So you're staying, then?" she asked.

"For the time being. I don't know for how long, but yeah, it looks that way."

She'd never told Georgia abut Lucy, and she didn't mention her now. It was a testament to her friend's faith in Mo's basic decency that she assumed Mo was staying for the sake of the kids, as Georgia herself would have done, in such a situation.

Privately, Mo hadn't a shadow of a doubt that if it weren't for the leverage her aunt wielded like a war-hammer, she'd be gone already. Roz had no misconceptions about her niece's nature. Damn her.

"It's getting late today, but I can drive you down to Cordelia in the morning. It's about thirty minutes south of here. We can rent a car for you there. I'd send you in my jeep but the idea of being stranded here without an escape gives me hives."

Georgia thought a moment, then said, "I get the feeling there's a lot you've left unsaid."

Sometimes Mo forgot that behind that pretty face, Georgia was much more perceptive than most people gave her credit for.

"I get that. This is your family, for better or worse, and if you want me to go, I will."

Mo shook her head. "*You* are my family."

And she had been since the moment Big Nick had made the mistake of patting Mo on the butt during her second shift behind the bar and she'd shoved him over the back of a chair. Georgia had laughed so hard her stripper make-up had started to run down her cheeks.

"Glad you find this funny," Mo had said, reaching behind the bar for her bag.

Georgia had stood up from her bar stool and helped the floundering man to his feet, chuckling all the while.

"Come on, now," she said. "Nick's not a bad guy, just awkward and dumb."

Although he was standing right there, Nick didn't disagree.

"Apologize," Georgia told him, drawing out the word as if he'd been an errant child.

"I'm sorry," he mumbled.

"Now run on back to your office," Georgia said. He obeyed, rubbing his own butt where he'd hit the floor.

The two women watched him go, then Mo slung her bag over her shoulder.

"Ah, don't leave," Georgia had said. "You'll just have to start over with another boss somewhere else. Why bother when you've got this one house-broken already?"

There was a certain amount of logic in that. Mo had stayed, and she'd made a friend for life. And Nick kept his hands in his pockets when she was around.

"If it's all the same to you," Georgia said, pulling Mo back from her thoughts, "I'll stay."

"You don't have to, you know."

"I know. But I'd like to. I have a feeling you could use someone in your corner."

They'd enlisted the help of the kids and Calvin and managed to get two rooms cleaned out enough that they'd do for the night.

"I'd offer for you to stay at my place," Calvin had said, "but I've only got the one bedroom."

"This'll work," Mo had told him, forcing herself to come to terms with sleeping under Roz's roof again.

"Roz certainly has the space," he'd said, as he helped her move a trunk full of God knows what. "It's just too bad she's filled it up with junk."

Aside from Roz's bedroom and the small room next door to it, where Iona was staying, Tate and the girls had taken up two more bedrooms down the hall. Mo was glad there were rooms on both sides of the house. She'd chosen two, one for herself and one for Georgia, that were as far away from her aunt as she could get.

That still left a large master that had once belonged to Rosalind and Calvin's parents and at least one more room that had always been locked, even when Mo had lived here before.

"Is this place for real?" Georgia had said when she'd stepped through the front door. "It's like a museum in here. Look at this stuff," she gawked, running a hand down a marble bust of some old, unidentified dead guy.

Even after they got two rooms cleared and found some reasonably clean sheets for the bed, not all of the awe had worn off.

"It must have taken years to collect this stuff," Georgia

said as she settled her now dusty, sweaty self onto one of the wicker chairs on the front porch.

Night had fallen while they'd been busy. The cicadas were singing.

"A lifetime," Calvin said, returning from his place with three bottles of beer. The kids had gotten hungry, so he'd fed them frozen pizzas and set them up on his living room floor with a movie and sleeping bags for the night.

He climbed the steps to the porch and passed a beer to each of the tired women, then flicked the switch for the bug light and settled himself down.

"Though, in all fairness, Roz had a head start. Our mother was the same way."

Mo took a long gulp from the cold bottle and watched the mosquitoes fly into the buzzing death trap overhead.

She'd never met her grandparents. She knew her grandmother had died when her children were still young. Her own mother rarely talked about her. Mo thought maybe Della didn't remember her well.

As for Matthew Mabry, Della had idolized the man. Idolized him in a way only the spoiled youngest daughter of a traditional southern family can manage. She'd called him *Daddy*, even as an adult.

And in the way of traditional southern patriarchs, he'd died of a massive coronary sometime in Della's teen years.

Mo had never heard Roz speak of him at all.

"And what did you think of my sister?" Calvin asked Georgia with a smile.

Mo's friend had insisted on introducing herself to their hostess earlier in the day.

"I can't sleep under the woman's roof without at least saying hello."

She wasn't in the room long.

"Well," she said now. "Let's just say, I can see where Mo gets her charming personality from."

Calvin laughed, and the corners of Georgia's mouth tugged wider.

As Mo watched them she couldn't help but see the way their eyes drew back to one another. She wondered if they'd noticed yet.

Probably so.

Calvin had at least twenty years on Georgia. Gray was starting to fill in his beard. But as her friend laughed again Calvin's eyes brightened, and Mo thought there had been worse things.

The ringing of a cell phone broke through the conversation. Georgia rose to fish it out of her pocket. Mo knew it was Jack O'Shea by the way Georgia's face darkened.

"Hello," she answered, turning away from Mo and Calvin and heading down off the porch steps into the darkness of the yard.

Calvin stood as well.

"I should get going," he said.

"Thank you for your help, Cal," Mo said.

"Anytime, kid." He looked like he might say more, but he thought better of it.

"I'll see you tomorrow. Goodnight."

"Goodnight," she replied.

He smiled at his niece and headed back to his place, leaving her alone with nothing but the ill-fated mosquitoes for company.

She could see the lights from Cal's guest house from where she sat. She'd need to find a way to deal with those kids. It was a daunting prospect.

Mo had actively avoided situations that involved kids in the past. She felt ill equipped for the task.

She sighed. Tomorrow was soon enough to figure it out.

Georgia's voice drifted toward her in the still night air.

"... Too late for that, Jack," Mo heard her say.

She could tell by the tone of her friend's words that Jack O'Shea was fighting a losing battle. Georgia was done with him, whether he was ready to accept it or not. Mo recognized the death knell of a relationship when she heard one. Life with her mother had taught her as much.

For the first time it occurred to her that Georgia and Della Mabry were similar in a lot of ways. Both were women who sparkled, owning their femininity in a way that drew a man in. And yet, too often men underestimated the strength that could lay below that kind of beauty, realizing too late that a woman who knows her own worth doesn't need a man who takes that for granted.

Mo wondered where Della was now. If she was happy. But the ache of that loss was an old one, familiar and tired. There was nothing new to be seen there, so she tried to put it away.

Being back here was getting to her.

She pulled a last swig from her beer and leaned her head back, closing her eyes.

Mo must have dozed off for a bit. She woke when she heard Georgia say, "Mo, someone's here."

She opened her eyes to see headlights coming slowly up the drive.

"What time is it?" she asked.

"A little after ten," Georgia said.

"Not exactly visiting hours."

She stood, waiting and watching to see who would get out of the car that had stopped behind her jeep in the driveway.

The woman who stepped out and into the light that fell from the porch was dressed in a drab brown skirt and white button down and her dark hair was pulled severely from her face in a low ponytail. But she was still beautiful.

"Abigail," Mo said, greeting the woman with a question in her voice.

It was difficult to credit the stories she'd heard just this afternoon. But what does batshit crazy look like, exactly?

"Mimosa? Mimosa Mabry, is that you?" It was a wary question, without enthusiasm.

"It's been a long time, Abby," she said, thinking there was only one reason that would bring Abby Fontaine out to Red Poppy Ridge, and it wasn't small talk.

"I'm here for my daughter," Abby said, confirming Mo's

suspicions.

Mo nodded, wondering what the hell she was supposed to do now.

"Come on up, Abby," she said, inviting the woman onto the porch. "We can talk."

"There's nothing to talk about, Mimosa," Abby said, but she made her way onto the porch all the same. She didn't take a seat.

"Is it true? About your aunt?" she asked.

The porch lights overhead threw shadows on their faces, but Mo could see now that Abby had aged. Or maybe it was the solemnity in her face that added years.

"It is," Mo said. "She's been hurt. She's bedridden." There was no point in lying.

"And you're here to care for her," Abby said.

"Not exactly," Mo replied, but she had no interest in dissecting her family dynamics for Abby Fontaine and left it at that.

"This is my friend Georgia," Mo said. The two women nodded to one another.

"I want my daughter back, Mimosa," Abby said, skipping the niceties and coming straight back to the point.

"Abby, I don't know if this is the right time to discuss—"

"There's nothing to discuss. She's my daughter, and I want her home with me."

Mo carefully considered her words before she spoke.

"There are some people who are concerned, Abby. About Emma. About her well-being."

The lines on Abigail's brow deepened, but when she spoke, her words were as precise as Mo's had been.

"I understand that," she said. "I do. I even understand why Ms. Mabry did what she did, bringing her here. But things are different now."

Mo couldn't deny that. A great many things were different.

"I'm taking my pills like the doctors say. And Rosalind's

in no position to make demands—" Abby cut herself off and took a calming breath.

As if speaking her name had conjured up Roz's familiar, Mo saw the hulking form of Iona standing behind the screen door, listening.

"Look. Abby," Mo went on, ignoring the woman she knew would carry every word back to her aunt. "It's not that I'm not sympathetic—"

"Sympathetic?" Abby asked incredulously. "I don't care about your sympathy, Mo. Do you still call yourself that? Mo?"

There was a derogatory note to the other woman's words that Mo wasn't sure she'd earned.

"I'm not asking for your permission. She's my child, and I'm taking her home."

"I think we should all settle down. It's late. Why don't you come back tomorrow and we can—"

"No," Abby said, her voice rising. "Where is Emma?" Abby took a step forward and pushed past her, clearly intending to search the house herself, calling for her child.

"Abby," Mo said, raising her hands. "If we could just—"

"I'm done talking about this, Mimosa. And frankly, it's none of your business."

The woman had a point. But Mo couldn't shake off the image of Abby stapling a dead bird to a note.

It couldn't have been easy. Staplers aren't designed to accommodate bird carcasses. Was she slow and deliberate as she did it, or gripped in a manic frenzy? And what kind of delusions did it take to bring a person to that place?

"Abby, I can't let you—" Mo moved to follow as Abby put her hand on the screen door. Iona had disappeared. *Fantastic*, Mo thought. She could have at least blocked Abby's path.

Mo stopped when she felt a small hand on her arm.

It was Emma, looking waif-like in a long yellow nightgown covered in tiny pink flowers. The girl said nothing, just looked at Mo, then toward her mother.

"You can't stop—" Abigail broke off when she caught sight of her daughter.

"Oh, Emma," she cried, kneeling and opening her arms to the little girl.

With no hesitation at all, Emma ran to Abby and threw her arms around her neck. Fitted against her mother, the child's eyes drifted closed and a sweet smile played across her face as her head rested against her mother's shoulder.

An unexpected wave of envy rolled over Mo. She looked away.

Yet her eyes were drawn back.

Had there ever been an embrace as full, as necessary, in the history of the world, Mo wondered. Every hug, from every child, was a precious thing, she knew, but this was something else. Mother and daughter, each achingly aware of what was at stake and the importance of what they were clinging to.

This was a homecoming.

And yet.

The enormity of the love Abigail had for her child was hardly a question. But Mo couldn't help but wonder if Abby's mind had the fortitude to carry that load.

And had she, Mimosa Mabry, any right to be the judge of that?

"Em, honey, Mommy's here to take you home," Abby was telling her daughter, gently stroking her hair.

Emma drew back and gazed into her mother's face.

As if sensing the unspoken question, Abby went on.

"You know how I was... I was *confused*, before? Well, I'm much better now. The doctors helped me figure things out, and now I can tell what's real and what's not."

Mo wondered if it were really that easy, as Abby continued to stroke her daughter's hair.

"And Mommy misses you. Do you miss me? Do you want to come home with me? Forever?"

Gravely, Emma nodded her head. And for Abby, that was

that.

She rose, pulling Emma to her side and facing Mo.

"Mr. Mabry," Abby said, inclining her head to Calvin, whom Mo hadn't noticed had joined them on the porch. He must have followed behind Emma.

"Abby, please," Mo tried again.

"No, Mimosa. This is my daughter. I appreciate what your aunt was trying to do, but it's not her place, and it's certainly not yours."

Mo looked to Calvin for help, but his face was as troubled as her own.

"Abby, I could call the police..." It was an empty, weak threat, and she knew it.

"And tell them what? That you've kidnapped my daughter? I know your reputation, Mo, and I pray you repent your wickedness. Because the Lord does not look kindly upon kidnappers, and I doubt the earthly authorities do either. I still have legal custody of my child."

Mo was tempted to tell Abby Fontaine where she could stick her prayers, but she struggled to hold onto her temper. Then Emma moved away from her mother's side and came toward her.

Mo knelt in front of the girl.

Neither spoke, but Emma smiled and put a hand on Mo's cheek, mirroring Mo's own actions from earlier that day. Then she turned back and took her mother's hand. The child's wishes were clear.

"We're going home now," Abby said, looking at Mo, Georgia and Calvin in turn, daring them to try and stop her.

There was nothing they could do but stand helplessly by as Abby and Emma walked past, down the steps, got into Abby's car and drove away.

Mo had never asked to be responsible for these kids. Lord knows, it wasn't a burden she felt prepared to face. But as she watched Abby Fontaine's taillights grow smaller in the distance, she couldn't help but feeling she'd failed.

"There was nothing else you could do," Calvin said,

reading Mo's face.

"Rosalind wants to talk to you," Iona's rusty voice came from behind the screen door.

Now you show up, Mo thought. She sighed.

"It's really too bad then, that I don't want to talk to her," she said as the taillights winked out in the distance. "It's been a hell of a day. I'm going to bed."

After a restless night, the morning dawned brighter than Mo felt was strictly necessary.

Lying on the lumpy bed with the blankets tangled around her, she stared at a crack in the plaster on the ceiling.

"I can go anytime I like," she told herself. "Just get in my jeep and go. It's my choice."

It felt like a lie, but it helped her to swing her legs out of the bed, all the same.

After a warmish shower in a spare bathroom that was in a sad and sorry looking state, Mo dressed and summoned the will to face whatever today would bring.

As she made her way down the hall, she saw Tate up ahead, looking furtive as he stood to one side of a window, watching something outside. Wondering what had drawn his attention so completely, she came up behind him and had to bite back a smile.

Georgia, dressed in a tank top and yoga pants, was doing Pilates, the morning sun shining through her hair.

"Pretty, isn't she," Mo said. Tate jumped.

"Sneak up on people much?" he spit out, unable to hide the flush that crept up his neck.

Mo, who hadn't at all snuck, struggled not to laugh.

"Hey man, I get it. If I were into girls, I'd be the same way."

Mo moved to walk past him and leave him to his pre-adolescent fantasies in peace, but he spoke again.

"Who hit her? Her dad?"

And what did that say about the kid?

Mo glanced back out of the window at her friend, whose face, scrubbed clean of make-up, made a fine canvas for highlighting the bruise that had deepened to a mottled purple.

"Boyfriend," she said.

"But why? She's so..."

Mo thought about it. She could feed him some line. But kids always knew when they were being patronized, so she didn't bother.

"I don't know, Tate. The best I can figure, there are some people out there that when they see something good it makes them feel so small standing next to it that they get mean. Then they try to smash it under their heel, so they can feel big again."

The boy thought about that for a moment, then nodded, accepting her explanation and turning back to the window.

Mo wondered what his story was.

She turned again, heading for the kitchen.

"Cal told us about Emma," he said.

She stopped and turned back.

"He said there was nothing you could do."

"And what do you say?" she asked.

"Maybe."

Damned by faint praise.

"And maybe not," he added, turning away from her.

Damned by faint reproach, as well, it seemed. But it echoed her own thoughts on the matter so closely that she couldn't hold it against him.

In the kitchen, she found Sadie watching Iona fill a tray with a steaming bowl of oatmeal and coffee.

"Morning," the little girl said to Mo, then gave all her attention back to the older woman, who was attempting to ignore her.

"Staring will do you no good, child," Iona said, her eyes never lifting from her task. "I take care of Miz Roz. I ain't no servant, nor no nanny."

Iona glanced over at Mo. "Besides, you got a minder

now. Roz still wants to speak with you, girl."

And with that, Iona picked up the tray and brushed past Mo on her way out of the room.

"I only asked her if I could have some, too," Sadie said forlornly. "Since she was fixing some already."

"Ignore her," Mo said. "She's was born an old bi...." Mo broke off, remembering at the last moment she was speaking to a child.

"Britches?" Sadie asked.

"I was going to say biddy," Mo covered.

"No you weren't"

Mo had to hold back a smile.

"I'm no expert," Mo said, changing the subject. "But I think I can manage breakfast."

Sadie perked up at that.

"French toast?" Her voice was full of hope and longing.

"Let's see what we have," Mo said, proceeding to rifle through the pantry.

After an exhaustive search, Mo and Sadie stared down at their bounty.

Two eggs, one of which had a crack running down the side, one packet of instant oatmeal, plain, and the heels of a stale loaf of bread. And a half-full bottle of gin.

"We can split the oatmeal," Sadie said. "I don't eat much."

"Who's been feeding you guys since Roz got hurt?" Mo asked in amazement.

"Cal's always got frozen pizza," Sadie said.

Mo sighed.

"Come on, we can do better than this," she said. "Go get Tate."

She went to get her bag.

"Should I bring the oatmeal?" Sadie called, holding up the packet.

"Leave the oatmeal. You two meet me at my jeep."

"Are you mad?" Sadie asked, leaning out the backseat of the jeep to talk to Mo as she loaded groceries into the car.

Mo smiled. "No. Not mad. Not at you. At myself, maybe."

"You're not supposed to talk to people like that, Sadie," Tate said from the front passenger seat.

"But they *were* old britches, and they were taking up the whole aisle."

"That doesn't mean you can say that. Old people don't like that. And the word's not britches, dummy."

"They moved, didn't they," Sadie said, dropping back down into the seat. "And don't call me dummy, you big dork."

Mo put the last of the groceries in the jeep, fighting back a laugh. She was digging in her bag for her keys when someone grabbed her from behind.

Without conscious thought, she reacted. Taking hold of the arm that was holding her, she shifted forward and down with all her weight, taking her assailant by surprise and flipping him over in front of her.

He slammed into the bumper of the jeep, then rolled to the ground.

"What the hell, Mo," the pile said from the pavement at her feet.

"Phillip?" Mo asked. She recognized her cousin's voice in spite of the adrenaline pumping through her.

She took a closer look, confirming that it was him, then reared back and kicked him.

"What is the *matter* with you? You can't sneak up on somebody like that!"

She kicked him again.

"Quit kicking me!"

"Oh, stop whining," she said, offering him a hand up. "I didn't even kick you hard."

"Nice to see you too, cuz," he said, once he was back on his feet.

Mo took a good look at him. He'd looked better.

"You're the one that grabbed me, jackass."

"Are you okay?" Sadie asked, breathless with excitement. Mo noticed two sets of wide eyes watching them from the jeep.

"Yeah, guys, everything's fine," she said. But Tate still looked suspicious. Sadie, if she wasn't very much mistaken, looked a bit disappointed.

"Phillip, what are you doing sneaking up on me like that? I could have hurt you," she said in a lower voice.

"You *did* hurt me," he said.

She raised her eyebrows.

"I know you're not waiting for an apology."

"I was *trying* not to cause a scene," he said, glancing around the half empty parking lot. No one was taking any notice of them, though.

"An outstanding way to go about it, chief," she said. "You know the cops are looking for you."

"That's why I was trying not to make a scene, genius," he shot back.

"Phil, if you didn't do anything, why don't you go down to the station and tell them that?" she asked in frustration.

He looked at her like she'd grown a second head.

"You're kidding, right. You think they're just gonna pat me on my head and send me on my way?"

She looked at him. Really looked.

"How many warrants do you have out on you?" she asked.

"At least two."

She shook her head.

"Minor stuff," he went on. "Some speeding tickets and this B & E thing."

"In what kind of alternate universe is breaking and entering considered minor, you moron?"

"It was nothing. Some storage units. Nobody got hurt!"

"Okay, okay," she said, raising her hands. "Calm down."

"Mo, if I go down there, they're gonna throw me under

the damn jail. They know I was there. Me and Nat. She gave us some stuff to sell."

"Gave you?" Mo asked. "You mean you took it."

"Yeah, all right," he said. "I needed the cash. But she was fine when we left, I swear to God. And now she's saying she can't remember what happened, and my ass is left hanging in the breeze."

Phillip shifted from one foot to the other and glanced around the parking lot again. In spite of his anxiety, still no one cared what was going on behind the red jeep. Mo wondered if anyone would've noticed if she'd actually been in any danger.

"I don't see that you have a lot of choices here, Phillip," she said. "This isn't a big place, in case you hadn't noticed. The cops are gonna catch up with you eventually. Just talk to them. Hiding like this makes you look guilty."

He shook his head, agitated.

"You've been gone too long if you think any of them are gonna believe a word I say. Mo, I need your help, babe. You gotta help me."

"Phil? Have you lost your mind? What do you think I can do about anything?"

"I need you to find Nat."

"Nat? Nat who? Nat Yates? What is that loser gonna do?"

"He was with me that night," Phillip said slowly, like she was an imbecile. "Keep up, Mo. We left together, then went down to the river to smoke."

She didn't need to ask what they were smoking.

"He's my alibi, Mo, and the dude is in the wind. I need you to help me find him."

She shook her head. "Again. What do you want me to do about it? I don't have the first clue how to find that guy."

"But you have something he wants."

"Flip," Mo said, reverting to the childhood nickname she'd given him many years ago. "You need to slow down on the smoke, buddy. I haven't seen that guy in a decade, and I don't have a damn thing that he wants."

She bent to pick up her bag from where it had fallen on the pavement and moved to the driver's side of the jeep, opening the door to get in.

"You do, Mo. Right there." He gestured to her jeep. "You've got his daughter."

Mo let that sink in, then glanced in the car at Sadie, who was playing with the cheap doll they'd bought in the grocery store. She wondered how much of this conversation those two had been able to make out. She sincerely hoped it wasn't much.

Slowly, she shut the door and walked back to her cousin, who looked desperate and jumpy there, on the hot pavement.

"You listen to me. Are you listening, Phil?" she asked.

"You— *We*," she said, jabbing a finger in his chest, "are not using a six-year-old girl for leverage, Phillip."

He frowned, then opened his mouth to say something, but she cut him off.

"Not gonna happen."

She stared at his face, watching the mutinous expression there.

"Nod your head, so I know you heard me."

He looked off to the right.

"Nod, dammit!"

Grudgingly, he did.

"Good."

Getting into her jeep, she turned the key. For a moment he looked like he was considering blocking her way. She revved the engine.

Finally, he stepped to the side. Throwing the jeep into reverse, she backed out, bringing her window even with her cousin as she did.

"What's happened to you, Phillip?" she asked.

If she'd expected him to answer that, she was destined for disappointment.

Mo put the car in gear and left him standing there, watching as they drove away.

"I don't like that guy," Tate said.

She realized that, of course, Tate knew who Phillip was. He'd lived with Roz for two years. She was the outsider here, struggling to bring together her memories with the reality of today.

"He wasn't always that way," she said quietly, almost to herself.

An image of Phillip rose in her mind. He'd had his own baggage, even back in the day, but he'd been a friend to her when she'd desperately needed one. And he'd still been clean with potential. She'd been the wild card, then. The one with dirty hands.

"Well, he's that way now," Tate said.

"Who's that?" Tate asked, as they pulled back up to the house.

There was a blue truck in the driveway and a stocky man arguing with Georgia in the yard. Mo recognized both the truck and the man.

"Boyfriend," she said.

"The one that hit her?"

"That's the one."

Tate reached for the door handle, ready to go out there and jump right into the middle of things.

Mo put a hand on his arm.

"She's got this," she told him. "Sadie, can you help Tate carry these groceries inside?"

In spite of her reassurances, Tate glared at the man, ready to drop the bags he was carrying and run to Georgia's defense given the least provocation. But Jack had his hands in his pockets and a hangdog look on his face as he tried his best to wheedle his way back into his girlfriend's good graces.

"Mo," he called when he spotted her. "Nice place your family's got here."

"It is. I don't remember inviting you, though," she said.

Jack shrugged, looking sheepish.

He must have gotten the address from Nick, whom she'd instructed to send her next paycheck through the mail. It wouldn't have been hard for Jack to talk Nick into giving up the information. Jack had an easy going appeal to him. That was what had earned him Georgia's affection in the first place. But gauging by her expression now, his charms had lost their potency.

Georgia's arms were crossed and she had a hard expression on her face that Mo rarely saw there.

Yep. Jack was officially the ex-boyfriend now, she thought. Mo helped the kids take the groceries into the kitchen, then settled onto the porch to watch what she hoped was the final act of the show.

"You had no business coming here."

"Aw, baby, don't be that way."

"Don't you *aw, baby* me, Jack O'Shea. We're done. Over. I don't know how many more times I need to say it."

"Have a heart, Georgie. I said I was sorry. I swear, it'll never happen again."

"You're right, it won't. Not to me, at least. Now get out of here, Jack."

"Georgie—"

Out of the corner of her eye Mo saw Tate join her on the porch, then did a double take at what he was carrying in his hands.

"Tate, put that away!" she said, jumping up and ushering him back through the front door.

"But she told him to go, and he's—"

"An idiot, I know, but you're not going to go waving around a gun," she said, carefully taking it out of his hands.

"But—"

"Look, he's sober, okay. He gets stupid when he's drunk, but he's trying to sweet talk his foot back in that door, not beat it down."

At least she hoped so, glancing over her shoulder at the two of them.

"Is this thing loaded?" she asked, breaking it open and

realizing that there were, in fact, two shells waiting in the chamber.

"What good's an empty gun?" Tate asked.

"Jesus," she said, removing the shells and leaving the gun against the wall.

"But—"

"No buts! Put that back where you got it, before somebody gets killed."

Mo pocketed the shells.

"Go on," she said, when he looked ready to argue.

Finally, he went.

"Jesus," she repeated under her breath, leaning against the door jamb to keep an eye on Georgia and Jack.

When Mo saw the brown and white SUV pulling up the drive, she wondered if Tate had called the cops before grabbing the gun, but that seemed unlikely. They must be here about Roz's attack. Or about Phillip, she thought.

But Jack couldn't know that.

"You call the law on me, Mo?" he called in her direction.

She shrugged. Let him think whatever he liked.

"I see how it is. I see. A guy can't even apologize," he said, moving quickly back to his truck.

"That's some hospitality, babe, I gotta say," he shot, then slammed the truck door and started the engine.

"That got him moving," Georgia said, joining Mo on the porch as Jack pulled out of the drive.

"Did you call the cops?" Mo asked.

"I thought you did," Georgia replied, shaking her head.

Jack was forced to drive his truck over the grass and around the SUV coming in. They watched the twin dust clouds that followed him as he roared down the drive.

"Here's hoping that's the last we see of him."

The SUV with an emblem reading Justus Police Department stopped in front of the house. A man in blue stepped out. He was wearing a cowboy hat, so Mo had to squint, trying to get a closer look at his face when he spoke.

"Mimosa Mabry. I heard you were back in town, but I

couldn't hardly credit it."

"Me either," she muttered, then her eyes grew wide when the man tipped his hat back and she got a good look at him.

"Wade? Wade Ashbrook? Is that you?"

"In the flesh," he said.

"Oh my God. I never thought I'd see you in a uniform. Except maybe an orange jumpsuit."

He grinned. "You're not the first one to say that, Mo."

"No, I expect not," she said.

Wade had been a friend, a good friend, she supposed, back when she'd been hell-bent on landing herself in a jail cell. Or a cemetery.

"Georgia, this is Wade Ashbrook. We were teenagers together."

"That's putting it lightly, don't you think," he said to her with a grin. "Why, what I remember is a whole lot more epic than that. Bonnie and Clyde. Calamity Jane and Wild Bill. Carter and Cash."

"Laurel and Hardy," she said. "And then there was Flip."

"She's being modest," Wade said it Georgia. "This girl's a legend around here, even after all this time. There was one particular incident involving a "borrowed" airboat, a bottle of Jim Beam and the city pool that's impossible to forget."

Wade grinned at Mo.

"Things might have turned out all right if Phil hadn't brought along the shotgun and the skeet thrower," he said.

As it was, they'd shared the back seat of a cop car often enough that seeing him there in that blue uniform was more than a little surreal.

"You're looking good, Mabry," he said.

"Thanks, Wade."

He'd always been a smooth one. The two of them had never gone there, but that wasn't due to a lack of interest on his part.

Of course, at sixteen he'd been interested in any girl who

walked by. She wondered if anything had changed, but there was a glint in his eye that said probably not.

By the time Mo had met Wade Ashbrook, she'd been wild, yes. Out of control even, some would say. But hooking up, casually or otherwise, was something she'd learned to avoid. She had trust issues, to say the least.

Red Beechum had seen to that.

Mo could still remember Red's reaction when she'd gone to him that last time. She'd been naïve, she'd been young, and she'd been scared.

When she'd left with Red's laughter ringing in her ears, she was more scared than ever. But not so naïve and never so young again.

"Is this is a social call Wade, or did the Chief send you out to preemptively arrest me?"

"He is gonna be *hot* when he hears you're back in town, that's for sure."

"You can tell him I've mended my ways. Haven't boosted any cars in at least a month."

"He'll be glad to hear it," Wade said, but then his smile faded. His face grew serious. "But no, I'm sorry to say, this is no social call, Mo."

"Is this about Phillip?" she asked.

"No," he said, shaking his head. "But if you see him we've got some questions we'd like him to answer."

Mo considered mentioning that she *had* seen him, just an hour ago, but she decided against it. What Phil ultimately decided to do was up to him. Mo didn't know where he was crashing anyway so she'd be no help to Justus PD, even if she wanted to be. And she wasn't sure she wanted to be.

"If it's not Phil, what's this about, Wade?"

He took off his hat and ran a hand through his hair, glancing away from them. Mo knew the look of a person about to deliver bad news.

"Your aunt's been caring for Abby Fontaine's girl, Emma."

Every molecule in Mo's body stalled. Georgia put a

hand on her arm and she saw fear on her friend's face.

"Ms. Fontaine was here last night. She took Emma with her," Georgia said, when Mo was unable to speak.

Wade nodded.

"I'm afraid I have some bad news."

Mo felt like her heart had been wrapped in rusty barbed wire. Any sudden movements would cause great and lasting damage. Wade looked like words had failed him.

"Say it, Wade. What's happened? Just say it."

"There was an accident. Abby's car..."

"Oh my God," Georgia gasped. "Are they okay?"

But Mo knew the answer to that before Wade shook his head.

"No, ma'am. They're not. Abby's car went into the river sometime last night. She and Emma... they're dead. They're both dead."

PART II

CHASING SMOKE

Three days later

"How was the service?" Roz asked from her bed.

Horrifying, Mo thought. She was standing at her aunt's bedroom window, gazing out at the garden where Tate was helping Georgia do whatever you do with gardens. He hadn't spoken to Mo in days.

The house was quiet and somber, with the gravity of where they'd been that morning hanging over them like a pall. Sadie was curled up next to Roz in her hospital bed, asleep.

"Fine," Mo said.

How could she describe the... the *offensiveness* of memorializing a woman who'd taken not only her own life but that of her child as well.

Because no matter what the official report said, Mo knew Abby's car hadn't gone off the road and into the river by accident. She knew it as surely as she'd ever known anything.

I've come to take you home with me. Forever, Abby had told Emma. Words Mo wished she could forget. There had been such commitment in her eyes when she'd spoken. Such love.

Mo had been the one to tell her aunt what had happened. She'd expected Rosalind to rage at her. To blame her, as she blamed herself, for letting Emma go, for not doing more.

But Roz had only closed her eyes, trying to block out—

in the only way available to her—the devastating news. Mo had waited, knowing she'd earned whatever Roz would throw her way. But she'd forgotten for a moment that this woman had a core of steel that even a broken body couldn't bend.

"Call Hayes," Roz had said quietly. "Arrangements need to be made."

Mo had nodded, moving toward the door. But she'd stopped.

"Roz, I…" I'm sorry seemed so inadequate. She struggled to find better words.

"I know, Mimosa," her aunt said.

There was no comfort there. For either of them.

Roz had paid for the private service. Had paid for the headstones Mo had chosen, too.

There was no one else.

And now that that was done, there was little else to do. Mo longed for something. Something else. Something more profound to mark the passing of a child she'd only known a day.

But here they were.

"You want to go now," Roz said behind her.

It wasn't a question.

Mo glanced at Sadie's sleeping form.

"I do. I want to go as far from here as I can manage and just as fast."

Roz said nothing. Only waited.

"But it wouldn't help," Mo said. "You can't outrun your own head. I've tried."

She turned away, not wanting to meet her aunt's eyes. There was nothing there she wanted to see.

"Someone's coming," Mo said, straightening.

She left Sadie and Roz, with a conscious effort not to run from the room.

"I can go, if you're not in the mood for visitors," Wade said when he stepped out of his car.

"I don't know what kind of company I'll be, but you can stay if you like. As long as you're not bringing more bad news. I don't think any of us can handle that right now."

He nodded, removing his hat and taking a seat next to her on the porch.

"That is, without a doubt, the worst part of the job," he said with a sigh.

"I can't even imagine," she said.

"It was a fine service," Wade said, echoing her earlier words.

Had there ever been a more inept word in the history of language than *fine*?

"I suppose it was," she said.

They sat in silence after that, listening to the birds call to one another in the trees.

"How long are you staying, Mo?" he asked.

She didn't know the answer to that.

"For however long I do, I guess."

"Calvin told me a little about why you're back."

Mo snorted. "To fail miserably at taking care of these kids? Yeah. I've done a bang-up job so far."

Wade shook his head.

"It's not your fault, you know."

"Yeah? You think if you say that out loud, it'll make it true?"

"Mo—"

"Don't, Wade," she said. "There's no point in lying to myself. If I hadn't sent that girl off with her crazy mother…"

"There was nothing you could've done."

People kept trying to sell her that line. But she was having a hard time buying it.

She knew the truth. And the truth was, even as she'd been telling Abby no, to come back the next day, she'd been thinking of herself. Thinking about her mother. Of being kept from her. Of being lied to. Separated.

Della wasn't even home when Roz had come and picked her up. Her aunt had lied, telling Mo that Della would come later, that she'd meet her here, at Red Poppy Ridge.

Mo had left everything behind, not knowing…

But Della hadn't been invited.

Roz had banned her from the house, from her daughter, and she'd kept them that way.

Apart.

Mo hadn't wanted to do the same, to keep a mother from her child. She'd seen the way Emma held Abby, with her eyes closed so tight, and she'd stepped aside.

And look what she'd reaped.

Georgia and Calvin stepped around from the side of the house, saving Mo from her thoughts.

"Wade," Calvin called from the yard in greeting.

Georgia stepped up onto the porch to join the two of them, but Wade stood, picking up his hat.

"Don't run off on my account," Georgia said.

"No, ma'am," Wade smiled. "I've got to get going anyway. Just wanted to drop by and see how everybody's holding up."

He donned his hat and nodded in Mo's direction.

"I hope I see you again, Mo," he said. "Under better circumstances, next time."

She nodded but made no promises she didn't know if she could keep.

Wade headed back to his car, stopping to shake Cal's hand.

The two women couldn't make out what was being said, but the men were obviously friends.

"Did you know your uncle grows pot?" she asked Mo.

"Yeah."

"A lot of it," Georgia said.

"Biggest supplier in three counties," Mo confirmed. "Unless he's expanded."

The way Mo understood it, Roz had inherited the big house when their father died and a third of the land. Calvin, the guesthouse and a third of the land. Della had received a forgotten amount of money and the final third, which she'd turned around and sold back to the others. Della was never the sort to settle down, though Mo knew her mother always loved Red Poppy.

When Roz had inexplicably declared her little sister unwelcome, the off-limits appeal of the place had grown to mythical proportions. At least, in Della's mind. Mo had never understood it.

As for Cal, he'd found a way to put his inheritance to a lucrative use.

"Does he know that?" Georgia asked, nodding her head in Wade's direction.

Calvin let out a laugh at something the younger man said and clapped him on the shoulder in a good natured way.

"He should," Mo said. "Cal's who we used to steal weed from when we were twelve years old."

Mo had existed in this place for a week of her four-week sentence before she'd snapped.

When a pile of old boxes full of useless junk had tumbled down in the hallway that she and the others had so painstakingly cleared, that was the last straw. Why Roz chose to live this way was a mystery she'd long since abandoned trying to figure out. But the idea that she'd brought not one but three children into such a quagmire was inconceivable.

Mo called in reinforcements.

"Roz isn't going to like this," Calvin said.

Mo knew that.

"Yeah? What's she gonna do about it?" she threw back at him.

They'd started in Matthew Mabry's old office. Mostly because the room was one of the few in the house that hadn't been hoarded. They moved the furniture to the walls and set up ground zero for sorting keep, donate and burn piles.

"Roz wants to talk to you," Iona had said from the doorway, several dusty hours into the job. Without waiting for a reply, she'd disappeared back into whatever shadowy corner she'd come from.

Sighing, Mo thought she might as well get this over with. "This is low, Mimosa. Even for you."

Ah. There was the anger she'd been looking for before.

"You want me to stay here and take care of these kids?"

"That doesn't give you the—You have no right—" Roz sputtered.

"This place is in no fit state to have these kids here."

"That's not your decision to make!"

"Actually, it is. And I made it. So I suggest you deal with it."

"Mimosa!" Roz called to her niece's retreating back. "You get back here, damn you!"

Mo could hear the frustration pouring out of her aunt's words as she walked away. There might have been the smallest grain of sympathy floating around inside of her for the woman who'd once been an unstoppable force of nature, but she ruthlessly stomped it down.

Kids had no business living in this mess. And the fact that Mo had always hated it too didn't dilute the truth of that.

"What are you going to do with all this stuff?" Georgia had asked, looking around them in amazement.

"God, I don't know," she sighed.

Things like broken lamps and old used car parts she had no problem getting rid of, but in spite of what she'd said to Roz, Mo wasn't completely indifferent to the innate value of some of this stuff.

There was just too damn much of it.

"Is there any sort of local historical society around here?" Georgia asked as she flipped through a box of old sepia-toned photographs.

Cal nodded. "It's run by Cecily Greenway. Roz hates her."

"Good," Mo said. "Call her. She can have any books, papers or photos of historical significance that you don't want, Cal."

He shook his head. "I've never felt the same way about this stuff as Roz."

"It's settled then. As for the jewelry, the antiques, the artwork that's not already on a wall, I'll call Hayes. He can set up an estate sale. We'll put the money in trusts for Sadie and Tate."

Calvin and Georgia both nodded, slightly mollified that they weren't accessories to pillaging Rosalind's home and possessions for personal gain.

"She won't like it, but she'll live," Mo said. "Why don't we take a break and make some lunch. This stuff's not going anywhere."

"I'll make some pizzas," Cal said.

"No, I'll take care of lunch," Georgia said. "You guys eat too much pizza."

"I like pizza."

"You just track down Tate and Sadie and meet me in the kitchen." Georgia abandoned the box of photos and followed Calvin out the door, leaving Mo alone in the midst of the mess they'd created.

Dropping down into her dead grandfather's office chair, Mo wondered what the hell she was doing.

Yes, the place needed to be cleared out. Needed it desperately, if it was to be any kind of home for kids. But that wasn't her problem, was it? Not once her month was up.

There was the upshot of angering her aunt. She couldn't deny the appeal that held.

But still, the process made her uneasy. It felt too much like settling in. And the idea of settling in here, in this place, angered her at least as much as Roz must be.

Suddenly furious at her aunt all over again and more so, at herself for being pushed into this in the first place, Mo picked up the first thing that came to hand and threw it at the wall.

The ceramic vase shattered into a dozen pieces.

The sound broke through her self-pity. She hated losing her temper, feeling that sudden slip of control.

"Get your act together, Mabry," she said under her breath, rising to find a broom before somebody cut themselves.

Sweeping up the pieces, she saw the vase hadn't been empty. Lying amidst the shards was a ring of keys.

Mo bent to pick them up, thinking there was nothing more useless than old keys, when you haven't the faintest clue what they unlock. She tossed them back onto the desk and turned to go.

She was halfway to the kitchen when a thought occurred to her that halted her step.

Keys in hand, Mo stood in the hallway in front of the room that had always been locked. She remembered trying this door once when she was a teenager, only to find it barred.

Mo felt the desperation of that time wash over her.

She'd been searching the house, leaving a slew of mess in her wake. But looking for anything in this place was like combing through a pile of needles for a needle, a useless act of defiance.

She'd been searching for letters. Her letters. The ones Della had sent that Roz was keeping from her.

She remembered her mother's voice on the phone.

"What do you mean, you didn't get them?"

And Mo knew, Roz was taking them, separating her from her mother in one more way.

"Give me my mother's letters," she'd demanded.

Roz leaned back in her chair and looked at her niece, standing there, going on fifteen with a growing belly.

If Mo had thought she'd deny it, she was wrong.

"No," Roz said, then looked back down at her own correspondence, dismissing her sister's daughter like she was nothing.

"You can't do this!" Mo had said. "You can't keep me from my mother this way."

She'd converged on Roz, but her aunt continued to ignore her. Reaching down and sweeping an arm across the table, Mo sent Rosalind's papers flying.

"I want those letters," she'd demanded, slamming both hands flat on the table and forcing Roz to acknowledge her.

"Having a temper tantrum will do you no good, Mimosa," she said, but her aunt's calm enraged her further.

She'd torn through the house, emptying drawers and cabinets, rifling through desks and dressers, to no avail.

Mo had been brought up short, here, in front of this door. It was locked then, just as it was now.

"You won't find what you're looking for in there," Roz had said to her.

"Give them to me," Mo had sobbed, leaning her back against the locked door and sliding to the ground. She'd cried into her hands, despising herself for showing this kind of weakness to her aunt.

It felt like exposing her jugular to a predator.

"Don't bother, Mimosa. You won't find any letters from my sister in this house. I burned them as they arrived."

"Why?" Mo had cried. "Why are you doing this?"

She'd asked the question before, and like before, Rosalind didn't bother to give her an answer.

"I hate you," Mo had said, her voice low.

Rosalind only looked at her, her back straight and unbending.

"Yes, I know."

Then she'd walked away.

Shaken by the memories, Mo hesitated at the door.

But Roz wasn't here to stop her now.

With purpose, she straightened her spine and began trying keys in the door.

The first eight didn't work. With a deep breath she looked down at the ninth and final key on the ring. She slipped it into the lock. But if she'd expected some sort of *Hallelujah* moment, it wasn't going to happen.

The knob didn't turn.

"Of course it didn't work, you fool," she muttered. "Has anything around here ever been that easy?"

With a sigh she backed up and looked at the door, the useless keys dangling from her hand.

Not this time, she thought, then turned and walked down the hall.

A few minutes later she was back, the keys abandoned for a screwdriver. She went to work on the hinges.

In a few moments time, there was a satisfying thunk as the door fell away from the frame and hit the floor.

Mo didn't know what she was hoping to find but the room in front of her didn't appear to be stuffed with the skeletal remains of her aunt's former victims.

It all looked rather... ordinary.

There was a faded rug that took up most of the hardwood floor, which had muted the fall of the door. There was a full-sized bed, covered with an equally faded quilt.

A dresser. A vanity that was surely an antique if the crackled glass of the mirror was any indication. And a door that, judging from the mundane contents of the room, no doubt opened on an ordinary closet.

There was nothing at all, at first glance at least, to warrant closing this space for years on end.

Mo slowly stepped into the stale air of the room. Her eyes fell on a piece of furniture she'd missed.

Backed up against the wall that the door was on, there it was. A crib.

Shaking her head at the incongruousness of it, Mo walked over, taking note of the pale yellow and gray bedding. The paintings of pudgy zoo animals on the wall above it.

She touched a finger to the mobile hanging above the child's bed. It moved slightly at her touch, giving off two tinny notes.

Mo moved to the closet, cracking open the door. There was an assortment of clothing hanging there. A woman's closet.

Or a girl's, she thought, noting the soft ruffled cap sleeves on a pale blue dress with white polka dots.

She couldn't imagine Roz wearing any of these clothes.

Her aunt must have been a young girl once, but even as a girl named Rosalind, her aunt had never worn this dress, Mo was sure of it.

No. These were Della's things.

This was once her mother's room.

Mo turned to look at the crib again. She'd known they'd lived here, for a time, after she was born.

For years, maybe. Before everything went wrong.

Roz had thrown them out, Della had told her, though she'd never explained why. But Mo knew it was true. She had those hazy memories of sunlight and laughter.

This crib was hers. It must have been.

Uncomfortably, Mo realized she didn't like this room. She didn't like the way it made her feel.

She'd gone to a fair amount of trouble to get in here, expecting to unearth some hidden secrets that Roz had locked away, unable to face, for whatever reason.

She'd never expected to find a piece of herself.

I'll close it back up, she thought, moving to the gaping doorway.

But the questions. The questions couldn't be locked away.

As Mo walked past the dresser her eyes landed on an object lying on top.

It was a picture frame that had been set upon its face.

Automatically her hand moved to set it upright but at the last moment, she stalled.

But it was past too late to turn back now.

She picked up the frame, and her breath caught.

It was Della.

Had she forgotten how radiant her mother was? The photo had been taken at just the right moment to capture it. Or maybe Della always looked that way. A photographer's dream.

She was young. So young. And she was laughing, the sun streaming through her hair, as she held up a baby to the sky. An offering to the gods of sunlight and spring.

The baby beaming down into her mother's face was Mo.

She ran her fingers down the glass of the frame, tracing the web of cracks where it had been broken at some point in the past.

An accident? Somehow, she thought not.

Mo gripped the frame in her hands.

Yes, this room had been Della's. Probably the one she'd grown up in, dreaming a child's dreams in that bed. It had also been a room she'd shared with her daughter for a time.

But in a more encompassing way, this room was Roz's room, too.

Mo's eyes fell on the door that lay across the carpet, then back to the cracks in the glass.

Roz had been the one to turn the key, to lock this all away. And she'd kept it that way.

Why?

Mo felt like an intruder into a hidden piece of her aunt's mind.

Still holding the photo, Mo moved out the door and made her way to her aunt's room. She could hear voices from across the house, but she didn't pause.

Thankfully, Iona was nowhere in sight. She'd left a television on in her absence, although Roz had her eyes closed to it. When Mo switched it off, her aunt opened them.

Judging by the alertness she saw there, Mo doubted the older woman had been sleeping.

She held up the photo in its broken frame.

Roz must know where she'd gotten it from, but in typical fashion, she said nothing.

"Why? Why do you hate her so much?"

The woman may as well have been a statue for all the emotion she showed.

Mo sighed. "Fine. Sit there and say nothing then. But people who don't care don't bother to lock things away."

Mo turned to go.

"I don't hate her," her aunt said.

Mo turned back.

"I see her for what she is."

"What is that supposed to mean?"

Roz looked away. She seemed angry now. At the mention of her sister, or at the fact that she'd spoken about her at all, Mo couldn't begin to guess.

"I don't know what makes you think I plan to start explaining myself to you, Mimosa."

Mo shook her head.

"No. I can't imagine. God knows you never have before."

There were footsteps at the door.

Georgia came around the corner. She looked breathless and upset.

"Ms. Mabry," she said, nodding in Roz's direction.

"Mo, have you seen Sadie?"

"No. She's not with you?"

Georgia's eyes darkened with worry.

"Mo, we can't find her. We've looked everywhere. She's... she's missing."

They searched again, with Mo's help, but it was no use. Sadie was gone.

Mo, Georgia and Calvin met up in the front yard, each coming from the different directions, each as empty handed as the next.

"Could she be with her parents? Maybe her mom came and got her the way Emma's—" Georgia broke off.

Calvin shook his head.

"Sadie's mother was a junkie. Left town when she was just a baby. Far as I know, nobody's seen hide nor hair of her since. She left Sadie with her dad. And Nat doesn't know much, but at least he had the sense to know he had no business raising a little girl."

"Mo—" Georgia said, her hand at her mouth.

"Don't panic," she told her friend, but that was a

worthless thing to say.

"Call Wade," she told Calvin.

They could hear Tate calling Sadie's name in the distance.

"And stay here. I'll be back."

She headed for her jeep, then changed her mind, switching directions back to the house.

Rifling through the front closet, she found the shotgun right where she'd left it. After a moment's hesitation, she grabbed the pair of shells she'd placed on the top shelf when Tate wasn't looking. After all, what good was an empty gun?

Georgia's eyes widened as Mo hurried back to the jeep.

"Where are you going?" Calvin asked.

The sight of the gun hadn't helped with Georgia's panic.

"I might be spinning my wheels, but I may know where to find her. Or at least, someone who does," she said, putting the shotgun in the floorboard behind the seat.

Tate emerged, running for the jeep and jumping into the passenger side.

"No. You're not going."

"I'd like to see you try and stop me," the kid said.

It only took one look at the stubborn set of his jaw to see he was ready for a fight. He had been since Emma had been found in the river.

And this was not a hill she had the time to die on.

"Fine. You do as I say, or I swear, I will skin you alive and leave your carcass for the buzzards."

"Just drive, already," he said, unimpressed.

"And buckle your seat belt."

Gravel crunched under her tires as she pulled into the parking lot of a run-down bar called Timberwolves. She'd say the place had seen better days, but she wasn't sure that was true. It must have been new once, but as far as she remembered, it'd always been a rusty old dive.

"Stay in the jeep," she told Tate.

"But—"

"Tate,' she said, pointing a finger at him. "This time, you do as I say. No buts."

And she meant it. It may be early but there were plenty of cars in the parking lot and the place wasn't known for its classy clientele.

Tate crossed his arms.

"Fine."

With a final stern look in his direction, she left him and headed for the door.

She couldn't stop the wave of familiarity that hit her as she stepped into the dimly lit bar, though she had no time to ruminate on the screwed up reasons she felt at home in places like this. Add partially naked women and Nick's was no different.

She'd grown up in this place, as much or more than during the years she'd spent with Della. But it was a little blonde girl on her mind today, not the lost girl she'd once been.

Mo made a beeline for the pool tables lined up along the wall. Leaning against a post, she watched the game and noted the players.

She wasn't disappointed. She recognized one for sure. Another seemed familiar. Under the beer gut and the receding hairline, she was almost positive it was Billy Early.

It didn't take long for the group to notice her. There weren't that many people in the place, and though her breasts weren't that impressive, they did qualify as breasts.

That was all it took.

"Hey there, pretty lady. Can I buy you a beer?" said one of the guys she didn't know.

They all turned her way, sensing fresh meat. Even the one leaning over a haggard woman in the corner.

"Holy mother of gawd! Mo Mabry? Is that you?" said the Romeo with the woman.

His girl looked less than pleased when he made his way over, as did the guy who'd spoken to her first. She supposed he thought he had dibs.

"Dave Brandt," Mo said. "Have you been sitting in this bar since I left town? I swear to God, this is the last place I saw you."

He laughed. "The rent's cheap, and the women are too," he said, earning a glare from the woman on the bar stool.

Dave grabbed her in a hug she wasn't expecting and threw an arm around her shoulders.

"Boys, this here's Mimosa Mabry," he said, showing her off to his friends like an oversized catfish.

"You, sirs, are in the presence of a goddamned living legend. Show some respect."

One of the men actually took off his hat and offered up his stool.

The introduction was out of proportion, to Mo's mind. She was no legend. She'd once been a girl with nothing to lose. Nothing more, anyway. That Dave made her out to be some sort of backwater royalty was a bigger testament to his own foolishness than to anything she'd ever done.

"How the hell you been, Mo?" Dave asked, although he didn't wait for a reply.

"Billy, you remember Mo, don't you, you fat lump of stupid."

"Yeah. Hey Mo, good to see you," Billy said, bobbing his head at her.

"Roy, get this lady a beer, why don't you. You just got paid."

Dutifully, Roy trotted off to the bar to procure said beer.

"Thanks, Dave, but I'm not staying. I'm looking for my cousin. Have you seen him around?"

"Phil?" Dave asked. "Yeah, I seen him. Sombitch owes me money."

"You know where he's crashing?"

Dave met the eye of a fourth guy who'd yet to be introduced.

"Naw," he said. "Heard he's hiding from the po-po."

"Among others," anonymous fourth guy added with a

smirk.

"Come on, Mo," Dave said. "Drink a beer with us. Play some pool. You won't find a better crowd around here, that's for damn sure."

Mo tried not to let her frustration show.

"What about Nat Yates?" she asked.

"What about him? He's not here. We are."

Roy, back from the bar, pressed a beer into her hands.

"I can't stay, Dave. It's really important I find Phil. Are you sure you don't have any ideas where I could track him down?"

Dave rocked back on his heels and tilted his dirty ball cap up on his head.

"Well now, maybe I do and maybe I don't, but one thing I do know is I don't know nothing for a girl who thinks she's too good to have a beer and play a little pool with the likes of me."

The whole situation made her want to break something, preferably the beer she was holding over Dave's thick head. But she'd already lost her temper once today. She wouldn't do it again for the likes of Dave Brandt.

She squelched the urge to scream and tilted Roy's beer up to her lips.

Chug-a-lug, Mo thought. She didn't have time to mess around with these guys any longer than she had to. In several continuous swallows, the beer was history.

Mo slammed the empty bottle onto the table.

Her audience started to whoop and holler, so she held up a finger. Then let out a belch that would make a roughneck proud.

Cheers went up all around.

Except for the Dave's forgotten date. She appeared unimpressed.

"Let's play some pool!" Dave said.

Mo nodded.

"Rack 'em up," she said, to another round of cheers.

A few minutes later, she'd run the table. The cheers had

given way to awe.

"I ain't never seen a girl shoot pool like that," Billy said.

"Course you have, Billy, you dumbass. The last time you saw Mo shoot."

"I must've forgot," he said, shaking his head.

Mo raised an eyebrow at Dave.

"Don't mind him. He took an I-beam to the head on the job a few years back. Scrambled the little brains he had to start with."

That was too bad for Billy, she thought, but she had other matters on her mind.

"Okay, Dave. Now give it up. You know where Phil's at or not?"

Dave had the good manners to look ashamed of himself.

"Actually, Mo, I don't."

"Dave. Jesus," she said, tossing the pool stick on the table and turning to go, regretting the time she'd wasted.

"Aw, Mo, don't leave mad."

"Piss off, Dave."

"Hey now, is that any way to—" he broke off when she didn't stop to listen. She was halfway to the door when he called to her back, "Fenton Gant. Try his place."

She turned to him. He had enough sense to look apologetic.

"If anybody knows where Phil's holed up, it's Fenton."

"Thank you," she said, with as much grace as she could muster.

"Don't thank me," Dave said. "Fenton's no fan of Phil's, from what I hear. You might want to practice your sweet talking before you go down there. It's a little rusty. For the record."

She lifted a middle finger to him as she headed back out the door.

If Justus' sweaty underbelly had a king, it was Fenton

Gant. Although Mad Hatter might be closer to the mark.

He presided over his twenty-four-hour tea party from an old metal building in the river bottoms south of the city limits.

The place had probably been a warehouse or an auto repair shop in another life, but now it was a mecca for lowlifes and tweakers.

And it never shut down.

Mo pulled the jeep over into the brush along the side of the county road. She threw it into park but left the engine running.

"Stay here," she said to Tate, emphasizing her words.

He looked ready to argue again, but she held up her hand.

"No. You shouldn't be within a mile of this pit. A bar is one thing, but this is different. These *people* are different."

His brow wrinkled.

"Maybe you should take the gun this time."

Mo hesitated. But the last thing she wanted was to make enemies here. She just needed to find Phil.

"I'll be fine. They know me."

Tate looked unconvinced.

The look didn't go away when Mo told him, "Keep your head down. If I'm not back in twenty minutes, take the jeep and go home."

His eyes widened.

"But I'm eleven!"

"Drive slow," she said, opening the door to get out.

"I'll be right back."

"Twenty minutes," he called.

"Twenty minutes," she agreed.

Mo walked toward the big roll-up doors that were peeled wide, letting the push of damp heat in and the smoke and tweaker sounds roll out, all tangled up together.

She'd mostly been talking trash when she'd told Tate these people knew her.

Some of them might. Fenton would. But prostitutes

and drug addicts had a short shelf life, and this had never been her particular patch of dysfunction.

Fenton Gant was a dealer and a pimp. But not a dealer in the way Calvin was. There was nothing natural in the stuff Fenton cooked up out here.

There was a big yawning room behind the mouth of the door. Some mismatched and used-up couches were off to the right, pointed toward a big-screen television with a confusion of wires hanging down.

A wolf-toothed evangelist was hawking Jesus there, from his multimillion dollar ivory tower. One of the bodies on the couch was prone, with an arm hanging down. The other, a guy who couldn't be older than eighteen, was drinking in the sales pitch, his eyes glazed and his mouth hanging open.

Maybe it'd be easier for the holy spirit to crawl in that way, she thought.

"John boy, turn that crap down already," came a booming voice from the left.

John boy gave a start. Around here, that was the voice of the only God a body needed, and John boy closed his mouth long enough to fumble around for a remote control. The sound went down, but the preacher's teeth still sparkled.

John boy couldn't look away from that shine.

"A bunch of leeches. Always a hand out for the hard-earned. Preying on folks, that's what they do. And what do they give you in return? Nothing but a worthless letter of recommendation to take to the boss man after you die."

Mo recognized Fenton. He hadn't changed.

He was standing to the left in a kitchen as fine as any up on the north side of town. A six-burner range snuggled in a marble countertop. High-end appliances shone as brightly as the preacher man's teeth.

Gant was a big man. A stand-up bass of a man, with a body fitted to the boom in his voice. Unlike the tweakers, who were wrung dry by chemicals and desperation, Fenton was a man who wore his excess proudly. A summertime Santa Clause.

"But I doubt you stopped by for a lecture on the evils of organized religion, did you, Mo."

"I don't believe they'd have me, Fenton," she said with a quirk of her lips. She noted the rows of closed doors that lined the second floor on either side of the big room. They each opened onto one of two long balconies that ran over their heads.

Mo had never been in one of those rooms, where, for the right price, all manner of itches had been scratched. She doubted any of them had exits to the outside.

"Oh, they'd have you all right. They'd snatch you right up, my girl, and pump Jesus into you harder than a green boy on his first old whore. Don't doubt it for a minute."

"Can't say I'm shopping for any religion, but I'll keep that lovely image in mind, in case I ever get the urge."

While he was talking, Fenton had filled two tall glasses with ice. Now, he finished squeezing fruit into a large pitcher of ruby red prettiness.

"You do that," he said, gesturing at her with a used-up lemon. He poured a glass for them both.

"Now pull up a stool there and tell old Fenton what you're in the market for today. Judging by the healthy glow you're sporting, the meth ain't got its nasty little hooks into you."

She shook her head, taking the offered seat at the pristine bar.

"That one's passed me by."

"And thank the big man for that," Fenton said, raising a glass. "I, for one, appreciate a woman with a glow. Too many toothless old scarecrows around here. Even the young ones. All wrinkled and deflated like old balloons."

Mo drank with him, to her health, her teeth, and her glow. Because when Fenton Gant offers hospitality it's best all-around to drink up.

Her eyes widened when the drink hit her tongue. It was like sipping a spring morning still wet with dew. At the look on her face, Fenton let out a laugh fit for a fisher king.

"Sheer beauty, ain't it," he said, lifting his glass to the light to admire his handiwork.

"It's the mint, see. A little mint, some hibiscus, and you got yourself some magic. And the rum don't hurt things none."

Mo couldn't resist another taste.

"Now, we've determined you're not here for dope, and unless I got you pegged altogether wrong, my ladies got nothing you want. So I'm figuring this little im-promp-tu visit has something to do with that cousin of yours."

"I was hoping you might know where to find him."

Gant nodded.

"Family matters, my girl. Nothing more important than family, is there?"

She shook her head in agreement, mostly because that's what he wanted.

"I hear ya. I do," Fenton went on. "But see, here's the thing. This here's my family," he said, gesturing all around.

She still only saw the two guys on the couches, but she knew there were more, tucked into the nooks and crannies. In those rooms with no exits. How many more, she couldn't guess.

"They're all worthless pieces of humanity, mind you, but still, I'm like their big old papa bear."

Fenton smiled, but he wasn't fooling her.

"And papa bear's gotta take care of his cubs, see. You understand, don't you Mo."

"I do, Fenton. I really do."

"Do you? See, part of taking care of this particular crowd of scramble-brained baby bears means taking care of business. And old Phil's put a wrinkle in my business."

Mo's unease, which had walked in the door with her and taken a seat, started tapping her on the shoulder.

"I'd like to help you Mo, I really would. I always liked you, girl. Trouble is, I been looking for Phil myself, and I ain't seen hide nor hair of him."

He could be lying. Phillip could be holed up in one of

those rooms at this very moment. But Fenton wasn't lying. He had no need to spin her a tale.

And that uneasiness went to tapping faster.

"Fenton, I sure do appreciate the hospitality, but I gotta get going. If and when I track down Phil, I'll let him know you're looking for him."

She rose from the barstool.

"Oh now, he knows. That ain't hardly in doubt. But don't run off in such a hurry, girl."

Screaming. Her old buddy unease was screaming in her ear now.

Gant raised a hand and made a quick come-on gesture with his fingers to some unspecified point behind Mo.

She turned and saw two men step out of the crannies she'd just been thinking about. These two didn't seem nearly so addled as the ones on the couches.

"Fenton, whatever Phil's done, whatever he owes you, I'm sure we can work something out. But I got to find him first."

She raised her hands, palm up, and took a slow step backward.

"Sure, sure. That sounds real good, except for one thing. I got this sneaking suspicion that Phil doesn't have what he owes me anymore."

She took another step backward, a step the cranny men matched frontward.

"That stuff is gone. I don't know why or how. Truth is, I don't particularly care why or how. But we both know that Phil don't have the cajones to run off with what's mine if he still has it to give."

That was a bone solid truth, if she'd ever heard one.

"And Mo, sugar, you know what that's called?"

Fenton didn't wait for an answer.

"In business, they call that a sunk cost. Gone and done."

He shrugged.

"Happens sometimes, you know. What can you do?"

When he smiled, a dimple showed up and she thought of the preacher, selling folks nothing for something, as long as that something was whatever coins you had in your pocket. And your everlasting soul.

"Then you went and made my day, sweet thing. Walking in here bold as brass knuckles. Because I had me a revelation."

"Yeah?" she asked, measuring the distance to the door, wide and free behind her.

"Oh, yeah. See if I could find Phil, I'd take what he owes me out of his ass. But I can't find Phil. You, on the other hand, with that healthy glow you got. Now, you're right here. And your ass will pay off a debt a lot faster than Phil's anyhow."

"Fenton, that's a fine offer, it is." She was stalling. They both knew it.

If she wanted out of here, she was gonna have to run.

"But I'm afraid I can't—"

Gant made another gesture with his hand, and Mo bolted as the cranny men came after her.

Mo really believed she had a fair chance until she saw three more men lined up at the open door. She skidded to a halt.

Slowly, they began to box her in.

"Fenton, I don't—"

"Back off," came a voice from the door. But if Fenton's voice was a bass, this one was more of a ukulele.

They all turned.

This kid. She wasn't in any position to complain, but the two of them really needed to have a sit down about his listening skills.

Tate waved the shotgun from one side of the room to the next. Mo had to fight the urge to duck when he did.

"You coming, or not?" Tate asked her.

"That's cute, kid," Fenton said to the boy. "But the grown-ups are talking. Put it down and we'll find you a popsicle."

Tate swung the shotgun in Fenton's direction.

Mo's feet finally found their go. She moved fast toward Tate before things got any more out of hand. The cranny men made no move to stop her.

"It's not wise to carry around a gun, boy, if you can't muster the spine to use it."

"We'll just go, Fenton," Mo said. "No hard feelings."

Mo and Tate backed up another step.

"Hmm," Fenton said, then lifted his hand again.

His men rushed at them.

Mo saw Tate squeeze on the trigger, and his future laid itself out for her to see, dominoes falling from this moment. Quickly, she reached out and pushed the double barrel of the gun upward, trying to snatch that first red domino before it could fall.

A shotgun makes an awful gut-shaking boom inside a metal building.

That ceiling's going to need work, was Mo's first thought. *Run, you fool, that was our chance*, was her second. But her feet had lost their go all over again. Or maybe it was her knees this time.

The cranny men ducked, but Fenton never did.

It was his big, swaggering laugh that filled up the echoes the shotgun left behind. It rolled and rolled some more.

"You there, boy," said Fenton, wiping the tears from his face. "If you ain't the pig's knuckles, kid. You get a few more inches on you and you come back to see old Fenton. I could use a man with balls like that."

The cranny men looked unsure what was expected of them at this particular point.

"Go on, then," Gant said, raising a hand to shoo them off this time.

"Get outta here, and be grateful I got a sense of humor."

They didn't wait for the big man to tell them twice. They backed out of that door in a hurry. Once they'd made it to the front of the building they broke into a sprint.

The jeep's engine was still running when they threw

themselves in. Mo tossed the gearshift into drive. In her hurry, she might have run the hooker down if Tate hadn't called her name.

"What now?" Mo muttered.

The woman standing in front of the jeep walked up to the driver's side with a nonchalance that set Mo's teeth on edge.

"If you're looking for Phil," she said, "try down at the river shacks."

"Why are you telling me this?" Mo asked.

"Cause that sorry sombitch said he's gonna take me with him. But here I am. And here he ain't. Try the shacks. And when you find him, tell him Destiny said to kiss her ass."

"Thank you," Mo said. This dried up piece of meat had delivered what she'd been looking for.

"You can shove your thank you where the sun don't shine, Mo Mabry. You get outta here now. Maybe you got a name still carries some notice, but you don't belong in the bottoms no more."

And thank God for that, Mo thought, as the woman named Destiny backed off into the trees and she could finally drive out of this place.

"You used to be friends with these people?" Tate asked.

"I was too young to fully grasp what a bad idea that was," Mo said, checking the rearview.

"Or too stupid," Tate said.

She couldn't argue with that.

The river shacks hadn't been used regularly since the days of the ferryman, but that didn't mean they'd been completely abandoned.

Plenty of locals had used the shacks for whatever deeds needed doing in the dark, ever since some enterprising person had cleared a path to them through the woods and down the clay riverbank. The shacks were still Mabry property, albeit along the opposite side of the river from the big house, but that had never stopped a soul.

It wasn't until Mo was seventeen, when Roz decided to fence off the woods and put up a locked gate that the nighttime traffic slowed down. And that was mostly Mo's fault. Though the police chief didn't come out of that matter entirely sterling either.

Pulling the jeep up to the rusty gate, Mo considered her options. She ought to take Tate back to Red Poppy first. It was less than a mile up the road. But they'd wasted hours on this goose chase. Evening was coming on. She couldn't help but feel the minutes ticking away.

She'd also come to accept the uselessness of telling him to stay put. In the end, Mo brought Tate along and left the shotgun behind.

"Forget it," she told him when he reached for it.

"That's a poor decision," he said.

"Maybe so, but that's the one I'm making, all the same."

The two of them climbed the gate, throwing their legs over and dropping down to the other side.

"What is this place?" Tate asked, his voice naturally dropping to a whisper as they made their way down the overgrown trail.

Mo hit the highlights for him.

"It's still accessible by boat, if you've a mind set on it, but it's been mostly left alone, so far as I know, for a lot of years."

The thick of the trees broke and they could see the river below. The roofs of the dilapidated line of shacks were visible, sitting in a little plateau along the riverbank that rose sharply on both sides.

"Ain't no trains crossing that thing any more," Tate said, pointing to the rusted out trestle bridge that precariously spanned the river some little ways upstream.

"Not for a long time," Mo said. She could see the sky clear through the places where the slats had long since fallen into the waters below.

Beyond the pine woods on the other side of the bootless bridge, the old red house stood, facing the other way, trying to pretend like this mess down here didn't exist. Like it didn't owe its original lifeblood to this place.

Mo could understand why the ferryman had painted the place red, stripping away that pretension. Because pretending like something didn't happen, didn't make it so.

Access to the train trestle had been gated off around the same time Roz had decided enough was enough with the shacks.

She and Phillip, and sometimes Wade, used to shimmy out onto that bridge and sit there with their legs dangling, drinking whatever beer they'd managed to sneak, or passing a joint if they had one.

They'd sit there and let the mosquitos eat them and watch the people who'd come and go below, thinking they were unseen.

It made them feel big. Bigger than any of them ever were.

Sometimes Mo still woke in the night, missing that ghostly feeling of her legs swinging in the air.

"Tate—"

"Don't give me that same talk, Mo. I'm tired of hearing it, and I'm not staying here."

She nodded.

"Okay, okay. I won't ask you to, but I need your help. I need you to have my back, like you did at Fenton's."

Tate stood up a little straighter.

"And you can't be my ace in the hole if I show them all my cards right up front."

"You want me waiting in the wings? Like a secret weapon?"

She nodded, hoping to God she wasn't setting up this kid's dominoes all over again.

"Okay, I'll stay outside, by the door. But we gotta have a code word."

"A code word for what?"

"For when you need me to come in, guns blazing. I should go back and get the gun."

"No," she hissed, grabbing his arm when he turned back toward the trail that led to the jeep.

"No guns," she said, shaking her head at him.

"Phil's not high on my list of favorite people right now, but he *is* my cousin."

She'd have happily shot Phil herself, given the chance, but she knew better than to speak that aloud.

"Besides, we can't risk it. Sadie might be down there. And if she isn't we're gonna need Phil to tell us where she is."

"To sweat him?"

She nodded.

"Yeah, to sweat him." Jesus H. What had this kid been watching on television?

"So what's the code word?"

Mo somehow managed not to roll her eyes.

"How about, 'Tate, come here.' Let's keep it simple, okay?"

"Yeah. That way you don't get confused. In the heat of the moment, you know."

Mo sincerely hoped she didn't regret this.

There were five shacks in all, lined up side by side. Like elderly women in a beauty pageant, each looked closer to falling down than the next.

As they got closer, Mo held a finger to her lips to let Tate know to keep quiet.

The two of them stood, listening.

There were noises coming from the second cabin. Apparently, Destiny's information was more reliable than one would rightly assume it to be.

Mo gestured for Tate to stay put. When he nodded, she crept along past the first cabin and stood by the open front door of the second.

"Gotta be here," she heard a voice say, then a sound like wood being stacked.

"I'm hungry. I want to go home," another, smaller voice whined.

Mo closed her eyes, a surge of relief nearly bringing her

to her knees.

Stepping quietly through the doorway, she saw Sadie sitting cross-legged on the floor. The man with her was on his hands and knees. He'd taken up several of the weathered floorboards and was blindly searching for something below.

Hearing her footsteps, he froze.

"Who's there?"

He was agitated. Jumpy. But Mo didn't remember him being dangerous. She hoped that was still true.

She stepped out of the shadows and into the light coming through the broken-paned window.

"Mo!" Sadie cried, jumping up to give her a hug.

"Mo Mabry? Is that you?"

"What are you doing here, Nat?" she asked.

"It is you! Well, I'll be damned." He sounded inexplicably pleased to see her.

"You didn't answer my question Nat. What are you doing?"

Nat rose, dusting off his jeans and shaking his head.

"Sorry, Mo. I can't stick around and visit. Me and Sadie, see, we gotta get out of here. I just gotta find it, and we'll be out of here for good."

"Why Sadie, Nat? Why'd you take her?"

"Oh man, I couldn't leave her with Miz Mabry. She's not safe there no more."

"Why's that, Nat? Did you do something? Were you the one that hurt Roz?"

His eyes grew big.

"What? Me? No, I don't know nothing about that at all," he stammered, but his eyes dropped down to the ground as he did. A blush crept up his face.

Mo thought he might be the worst liar she'd ever seen, and she'd seen a few.

"You weren't there that night?" Mo asked.

Nat was shaking his head no, but the voice that spoke came from behind them.

"Ah, she already knows we were there. I done told her."

It was Phil.

"Did you go back? After? Did you go back for more and hurt my mama, Nat?"

Nat's eyes swung between Mo, with Sadie at her side, and his friend. His confusion was hard to miss.

"Hey man, I… No. No!"

"Tell the truth!" Phillip yelled, his voice ricocheting around the small space and making them all jump.

Sadie held tighter to Mo's leg.

"Phil, man, you know I didn't do nothing," Nat pleaded.

Phillip fumbled in his pocket. Mo should have seen it coming. It'd been that kind of day.

"Tell the truth, Nat," Phil said, waving a small black handgun around.

Nat raised both hands, as shocked as Mo.

"Phil, man—"

Things got out of hand fast after that.

Sadie was no longer at Mo's side.

She tried to grab the little girl, but Sadie had put her heart into it and Mo caught nothing but air as the child hit Phil's side.

The gun fumbled in Phil's hands, going off with a sharp blast.

Everyone ducked, including Phil, who looked as taken aback as the rest of them.

"That's my daddy!" Sadie yelled, pummeling Phil with tiny flying fists.

Phil backed away like there was a pack of wasps coming after him.

"Sadie, Sadie!" Mo said, grabbing her. "Sweetheart, please, *please* go wait outside for us, okay?"

Her angry face calmed but only by a degree.

"You promise you won't let him shoot my dad?" she asked.

"I promise, love," she said with a forced smile and a stroke to the blonde head.

"Okay, then, if you promise."

And with complete faith, she walked out the door.

Mo's smile dropped away as she turned on her cousin.

"What is the matter with you?" she said, advancing on him. "What are you doing with a gun, you moron?"

She backed him into a corner, her finger punctuating her words into his chest.

"I didn't mean—"

"You could have killed somebody!"

Nat saw his chance and took it, bolting past them for the door.

"Nat," Phil called, pleading. "Nat, come back. I wasn't gonna use it."

Phil pushed Mo aside and went after him.

"Nat man, I need your help. They think I did it!"

Mo followed the two men out the door.

She could see Phil heading off to the left, presumably after Nat.

"Sadie," she called. "Tate!"

They weren't anywhere in sight.

Mo could only hope they were together, heading back to the jeep and away from those idiots.

"You've got to tell them, brother," she heard Phil yell. "You've got to tell them we were together. My mama, she doesn't remember nothing, but you do, man."

But Mo's biggest concern wasn't Phillip, or his alibi, which sounded shaky, at best.

"Sadie!" she called again, heading back to the right, up to the trail she and Tate had come down.

She could still hear fumbling and yelling as the two men tried to make their way through the thick brush up the steep riverbank on the far side of the cabins.

Ignoring them, Mo ran up the trail, searching for the kids. The day had grown dimmer, but the sun was still hanging on for a final curtain call.

Then Mo heard a scream. A sound like a bear crashing through the woods, though there hadn't been any bears to crash through this place for half a century.

The only sound more terrifying than a scream in woods full of creeping dark is when that scream cuts short, leaving a pregnant silence in its wake.

"Tate! Sadie!"

Frantic now, Mo had no thoughts left but to keep those two safe.

She might have passed them in her haste, if Tate hadn't stepped out into the trail.

"Mo," he said.

He was holding Sadie, whose face was buried in his neck.

She dropped to her knees in front of them, needing to touch them both, making sure they were there, whole and real.

"Are you two okay? Are you hurt?"

They both shook their heads, though Sadie didn't lift her face. Tate looked a shade past milk.

Mo grabbed them both in a fierce hug.

"I was coming to help. I heard the shot and I was gonna help, but then Sadie came out the door and then the others... So we came up, out of the way."

Tate was rambling, hardly taking a breath.

"Shh..." she said.

"I saw him fall, Mo. Sadie was looking the other way, but I saw him."

She didn't know if Tate meant Phillip or Nat, but she didn't wait around to find out.

"Get back to the jeep. Both of you. Lock the doors and stay there until I get back."

When Tate nodded, Mo ran back down the trail, skidding to a halt in front of the cabins. She scanned the area, then spotted him there, standing on a narrow spit of land at the edge of the woods.

It was Phil. He was looking down over the edge.

There was a drop there, straight down to the river below. It must have been thirty feet.

The bottom was lined with rocks. Rocks and the busted body of Nat Yates.

Mo made her way to Phil, careful about her step. It took some time, but Phillip's breathing was still heavy when she got to him.

"It was an accident." He was panicking, in shock.

"I swear to God, Mo. He came at me, after the gun, but I wasn't gonna use it. I just brought it to scare him, because I thought he was gonna run, and I needed him to stay. I needed him to stay and get my back."

He was rambling as badly as Tate, but he'd get no comfort from her.

"Jesus Christ, Phillip. Jesus Christ!"

"Without Nat, Mo, I got nothing. I got no alibi. Roz can't remember, and the cops are gonna pin it on me. They're gonna pin it all on me."

She looked at Phil, then down at Nat's body. His neck was turned at an unnatural angle as he lay across the rocks.

She could hand Phil some lie about it all being okay, but she knew it wouldn't help.

So she said nothing.

"I gotta get out of here. Please, don't tell them I was here, Mo. Please! Without Nat, I got nothing—"

She shook her head, cutting him off.

"Then you better run, Flip. Because I don't have a choice. I won't lie for you. I won't lie for anybody. I have to call the cops, and then I have to figure out how to tell a little girl her daddy's dead. So if you're not gonna turn yourself in, you better run."

And with the last of the light sinking below the edge of the world, he did.

PART III

MAMAS, DON'T LET YOUR BABIES

It was late. Mo was tired and she was angry.

The police had finally left. The paramedics had pulled Nat's body from the river. They'd had to bring boats to get him out.

And the questions. The endless questions.

Accident or not, they had to be asked. Mo had answered.

She hadn't heard if they'd found Phil yet. She couldn't imagine he'd get far. But she didn't much care either way.

Sadie was home. Tate was home. Both safe in bed. The same bed, Sadie needing the reassurance she wasn't alone.

With that worry sated, the anger had come to fill the gap.

Mo walked into the room where Roz lay, unmoving through it all.

"Enough," she said. "Enough with the secrets and the lies. A man is dead. You need to tell me what is going on. Did Phillip and Nat do this to you?"

"I don't remember."

"Bullshit." Mo didn't yell. She had nothing left over for that. "You're hiding something. You're always hiding something."

"You've got her pegged," said a voice behind Mo.

She turned in surprise.

It was way too late for decent people to be out. But Mo doubted this man had ever qualified as that.

Leaning against the door jamb, Arlo Vaughn had a pent-up air about him. Like he was itching to break loose.

"What are you doing here, Arlo?" Roz asked.

A fine greeting for a man you'd once shared a bed, a name, and still shared a son with.

The toothpick in Arlo's mouth jumped up and down, and he lifted a ropy, tanned hand to retrieve it.

"Rumor has it, you're on death's door."

"I wouldn't count on it."

"I want what's mine, Rosie," Arlo said, without raising his voice or losing the dance-hall smile off his face.

Mo thought they both might have forgotten she was there, as intent as each was on the other.

Without looking her way, her aunt proved her wrong.

"You can go now, Mimosa," Roz said, her eyes locked onto Arlo.

Mo opened her mouth but could find nothing to say to that, so she shut it and walked out the door.

She stopped outside to listen. It made her feel sneaky and small to do it, but she pushed that down.

"It's gone," she heard Roz say. "It was gone years ago, you stubborn old fool."

"Don't believe you."

"That hardly signifies."

"It does if I start talking about things. Things you'd rather stay buried. The truth about your baby sister, for one."

There was a pause. Mo didn't need to see her aunt's face to picture the look she'd find there. Roz had never been one to give ground under threats.

"You know, Rosie. I don't understand you. You had a chance to be a mother already. Taking in strays doesn't make up for that cock-up."

"Go ahead, then, you old bastard. Talk. Talk about any

damn thing you please. Talk all day long. But it's not gonna gain you a solitary thing. I already told you, it was gone so long ago, it's like it never was. Smoke in the wind. When are you gonna give it up, Arlo?"

"I ought to put you down, once and for all. You got a black heart, woman."

In spite of the threat, he never lost his conversational tone.

"I wish you would, Arlo. Some days I wish you would. But I'm not gonna hold my breath. You don't have the balls."

There came the unmistakable sound of a slap. It startled Mo, and she put a hand to her mouth.

But Roz just laughed.

"Is that the best you've got, boyo? You'd think you'd have improved your swing by now."

With his ex-wife's laughter chasing him, Arlo stormed out of the room, his face dark as he brushed past Mo without a word.

She watched him go the way you watch a snake crossing your path.

This wasn't the first time Arlo had shown up unexpectedly. Mo remembered meeting him when she'd lived here before.

He'd been friends with Red. As her belly had grown, she'd long since put away any naïve thoughts of a future with Red Beechum.

But Arlo couldn't know that.

He'd once shared his two cents on the matter.

"Men can't be trusted, honey. Everybody wants something. Some men more than most. And only one thing's for sure and for certain. The only person who ever wants what you want is you."

Roz called to her.

"Mimosa, send Iona to me, please."

She'd known Mo was there listening the whole time.

The peace and quiet of the next morning were at odds with Mo's state of mind.

Holding a steaming cup of coffee, she stared unseeing out the kitchen window at the bright day.

Sleep had given her tired brain a chance to shuffle through the confusion of the day before, dismissing the chaff and leaving only questions behind. She'd woken with those burning bright as flame.

Who had attacked her aunt, and why? What did Arlo want from Roz? What was the secret about Della he'd spoken of?

And hotter and deeper than the rest, did any of that matter next to the real question. The one that never left her mind.

What was the truth about Lucy?

Without any immediate answers, Mo's thoughts turned to the past before she could stop them.

She remembered the heaviness of her pregnancy growing apace with her unhappiness. Roz was no doting relation, even then. There was no warmth to be had in this red house. Just a deliberate and calculated distance between her and her mother, that seemed to grow wider with each passing day.

But short of cutting off her phone, a step even Roz wasn't ready to take, her aunt couldn't stop Mo from dialing the number she knew by heart.

Della promised she'd be there for the birth of her grandchild. Come hell or high water, she'd said. Roz wouldn't stop her. She'd be there, then she'd take them both away. Things would be like they'd been before, if Mimosa could only find the patience to wait.

It was a far off flickering light that Mo clung to during those long months.

And eventually there came the first clutching pains of labor. Mo remembered the panic and the need to reach out to her mother, to let her know it was time.

Squeezing her eyes tight, Mo made a concerted effort to

get off that train. It was barreling to a place she'd been before and didn't care to revisit.

She set her half empty coffee cup on the counter harder than necessary. She needed to get out of this house.

Sadie and Tate had been quiet today. Shaken, still, she didn't doubt. After a nearly silent breakfast, they'd wandered their way to Calvin's place.

She found them all on Cal's small front porch. It surprised Mo to hear Sadie cooing over a whiskey box.

"Come see what we've got," Georgia said, when she saw Mo walking up, but Mo didn't need to look. The mewing sounds that came from the box gave its secrets away.

"Look at it," Sadie breathed, lifting a delicate gray and white ball of fluff and holding it to her cheek.

If there was any more potent medicine for a six-year-old girl than a box of kittens, Mo couldn't think what it might be.

"Mrs. Perkins was down at the Save-Way this morning, giving them away."

"So you brought home the whole box?" Mo asked with a smile.

"They're kin," Tate said.

Mo supposed that answered that.

"They're hungry," Sadie said. "Should we make them a pizza?"

"Kittens don't eat pizza, dummy," Tate said.

"What do you know," she replied as she held one of the kittens up to rub noses with it. "Everybody loves pizza."

"I don't know if they're ready for pizza yet, but I'm pretty sure I saw some cat food in the grocery bag. Should we make these little guys some breakfast?"

"Okay. But I'm gonna name this one Pepperoni," Sadie said, with a nod of her head.

"Here," she said, thrusting the ball of fluff at Mo, then heading off to the kitchen with Georgia.

"That's dumb," Tate called, rising to follow them. "What are you gonna name the others? Sausage and Canadian bacon?"

Mo raised the kitten and met its blue eyes.

"Could be worse," she said. "You look more like an Anchovy to me."

The little cat opened its mouth wide and mewed at her.

She gently placed it back in the box with its two siblings.

"Arlo came by last night," she said to Calvin.

"Arlo Vaughn," her uncle said with a shake of his head. "Figured he was dead by now."

"He wants something from Roz. You have any idea what he's after?"

"Same thing he's always wanted. Wants his money."

Mo paused a beat.

"You're not telling me that old bank robber story's true?" she said, incredulous.

Calvin raised an eyebrow at her.

"Whatever gave you the idea it wasn't?"

"I don't know... Roz always said—" She stopped at the knowing look on Cal's face.

"And what's the single thing you've learned about my sister, Mo?"

"That she's a liar."

Calvin had the good grace not to nod his head in agreement.

"But then, how did he and Roz—" Mo shook her head. "I just can't see it."

"Arlo didn't always wear his vices as clearly as I imagine he does now," Calvin said. "Best I can tell, Roz figured herself in love with him."

"In love," Mo said. The idea was... difficult to wrap her head around.

"And he played her good. She left everything and everybody to run off to New Mexico with him. Some grand scheme of his or other, took him out there. Gone about six months, she was. But once she realized she'd hitched her wagon to a con man and a thief, against our daddy's wishes, at that, she packed her bags and came home. Though not empty handed, according to him."

Calvin shook his head.

"It must have been tough, swallowing her pride like that. But you'd never know it. She kept her back straight and her head high. She took back the name she was born with. If it weren't for Arlo following her back here after whatever he was up to went bust, then showing up at Red Poppy once every few years to harass her, you'd have never known it happened at all."

"But Phil…"

A darkness passed Calvin's face.

"Phil came along later. That was after our daddy passed."

"She got back together with him?!"

Mo had a harder time seeing that than she'd had picturing Roz in love. In her experience, once the woman set her mind on something, she never looked back.

"I never said that."

There were a lot of things that could mean. None of them good.

"Phil's the spitting image of Arlo, isn't he?"

Mo nodded. That couldn't be denied.

"Maybe that's why she couldn't warm to him."

"Do you think Arlo could've been the one who attacked her?"

Cal shifted in his seat.

"Twenty, thirty years ago, yeah, sure." He shrugged. "But that seems like a long time to wait."

"He threatened to spill some secret about Della. You know what that's about?"

"My baby sister has always been an absurd mystery to me. I find I'm happier that way."

Mo sighed and leaned forward, propping her elbows onto her knees as she gazed off at the green that surrounded them.

"I'd hoped you'd find a way to be happy too, Mo."

"I *did*," she said.

"Then why are you tossing it away at my sister's beck and call?"

Mo swung her head around to glare at him, then swung it back.

"You know why, Calvin."

"Can't you let it go, Mo?" her uncle asked quietly.

Calvin sighed.

"I know you hate her Mo, and Lord almighty, I can see your point."

"I need some answers, Cal."

"Maybe you're asking the wrong person."

"What does that mean?"

"If you really want to know, then I think you already got the answer to that. I think you always have."

"Were you here, Cal? The day my daughter was born?"

"No," he said.

But he wouldn't meet her eyes.

It was close to lunch time when Mo watched from the porch at Red Poppy as Wade's car pulled away. He'd come when she'd called, and she wondered if he'd be able to come through for her. She'd never asked a policeman for a personal favor before, and she didn't know how it was supposed to work.

"What'd you say to the cops, Mo?"

Mo turned to see Phillip. He'd been hiding. Watching, she guessed.

"Why the hell are you still skulking around here, Phil?"

"What else am I supposed to do?"

Mo shook her head. Had he always been so stupid?

"I don't know, Phil. Damn. If you're gonna hang around, you might as well turn yourself in."

"You can't trust the cops, Mo. Even Wade, man. Never

trust the cops."

"Then get out of town, moron. Before they find you. Because they will find you. You're not exactly a criminal mastermind,"

He looked like he'd slept under the porch. Maybe he did.

"How far you think I'd get? Gant's all over me for his money, and I ain't got it. That's why I was here that night. I just needed a little help."

"Do you want to see her?"

"Hell no," Phil said. "She doesn't want to see me anyway. She still can't remember anything?"

"That's what she says. If she did, surely she'd get the cops off your back."

"Hmm. Maybe."

"You think she's holding out on purpose? That's kind of low, even for Roz. You do something to set her off?"

"No. I mean... No, I don't think so. I don't know."

Phil ran a hand down his face.

"Look, just don't go running your mouth to the cops, Mo. That'd be a real bad idea."

Mo turned to look him in the face.

"Are you threatening me, Flip?" she asked slowly.

"No. No. Just... shit. I gotta go."

"I think that'd be best."

The county fairground was a piece of land that defied time. Nearly two centuries before it had played host to an unlucky group Mexican soldiers who'd fought and lost under General Santa Ana at the Battle of San Jacinto.

According to local historians, the prisoners had been treated kindly. Mo wondered if anyone had bothered to ask the Mexicans their opinion before that little piece of history had been written.

The same pen had decreed the treatment of German

prisoners of war over a century later as both humane and dignified, when the place served again as a POW camp during the devastation of World War II.

Since then, the quiet, unassuming piece of dirt hibernated, unseen and all but forgotten until it was called upon.

For the last fifty years, that time came only once a year, as the place woke from its rest to host the stink and the sweat of the annual rodeo and the carnival that came along with it.

Rolling into town from everywhere and nowhere, the big trucks coughed exhaust and noise, circling the fairgrounds like old dogs searching for the right place to rest.

When they found it and the trucks killed their engines, the carneys poured off like fleas.

In a matter of hours, the bones of rickety machinery began reaching skeletal fingers up into the sky, grabbing for the sun to snuff it out. Because it wasn't until nightfall that the carnival could truly come alive.

Under the cover of darkness, the thousands of flashing lights and the calliope music played their own shell game, directing your eyes only to the prize.

The screams from the roller coaster blended with the taste of fried foods and the musty smell of penned animals.

It was a unique and delicate kind of sorcery, pulling the stars from children's eyes and the cash from their parent's pockets.

In spite of recent events, Tate and Sadie weren't immune to the lure.

With strict instructions to stay within sight, they ran ahead, thirsty to drink it all in.

Mo and Georgia kept up at a more modest pace.

"You're brooding," her friend said once the kids were out of earshot.

It was true, and all the more noticeable in a place like this.

Mo sighed.

"I don't know what I'm doing, Georgia. I never thought

I'd be back in this place."

They both knew she didn't mean the fair that had greedily swallowed them whole.

"We can leave. Any time you're ready," Georgia said gently.

She was right. Mo knew she was. But her apartment with no pictures on the wall, the bar at Nick's, it all felt so far away. A hazy lifetime away.

"Don't think I don't consider it every single day. I'm letting Roz keep me here, while she dangles this knowledge out in front of me like a poisoned apple."

Georgia just looked at her, sympathy evident in her face.

Mo watched Tate and Sadie as they fished plastic ducks out of a baby pool up ahead. The tent was dripping with a stuffed menagerie. The ducks looked like they'd been through a war. She could sympathize.

"Calvin told me to let it go. But I can't, Georgia. Not until I know the truth."

Mo scoffed to herself, agitated.

"That word, *truth*. I've never been so afraid of anything in my life."

Georgia's brow wrinkled in concern.

"What if it's all bullshit? What if the truth's nothing but another pack of lies to get me back here, and the only truth out there is the same awful truth I've always had? That my baby's dead. She's always been dead. She only ever lived inside of me."

Georgia pushed a breath out between her teeth.

"Holy Jesus, Mo."

"I'm sorry," Mo said, scrubbing at her face.

After a moment, Georgia said, "I don't have any answers for you. I'm hiding out in the sticks *with* you instead of dealing with my own mess. But I do know one true thing."

"Yeah?"

"Those two, up there? For however long you choose to be here, their lives will be better for it."

Mo shook her head.

"Somehow, I doubt that."

"Doubt it or don't, it's a fact. And you know what else?"

Mo glanced at her friend.

"Yours will be too."

"He's not going to press charges," Wade said.

"Am I supposed to get down on my knees and thank the son of a bitch?"

"Look, Mo, I don't know if you realize how lucky you got. You busted the guy's nose."

"That guy was putting his hands on an eleven-year-old kid."

Mo hadn't heard what Tate had said, if anything, to provoke the man, and she didn't care. All she knew was one minute Tate had been laughing, running with Sadie back to them after having his bones jarred on the Cosmic Fury—his face shining in the multi-colored madness of light and sound. In the next minute, he'd seen something that brought him skidding to a halt.

Or someone.

"Did you see me?" Sadie asked, her blonde curls sticking to the sides of her face, plastered there by sweat and sheer joy.

"I saw you. No hands, huh. You nearly scared me to death." Georgia ruffled the girl's hair.

"Tate dared me, but he—"

Sadie broke off when she realized Tate was no longer right beside her. Turning, she followed Mo's gaze.

"That's his mama," the little girl said.

Tate was standing in front of a couple. The man wore a dirty John Deere ball cap and a paunch that pushed down his jeans so his thick leather belt had to work twice as hard. He could've been any of a hundred men around here. But the woman. She could see the mousy resemblance there.

Mo kept back, out of respect for a family she knew little

about, but her eyes never left Tate. She lost track of what Sadie and Georgia were saying.

"Mm," she murmured, when one of them asked her a question she didn't hear.

"I said, don't you think we should introduce—"

But Mo didn't hear the rest of the question. When beer paunch raised his voice and grabbed Tate by his skinny arm to shake him hard enough that the boy's head snapped back, she was moving.

Mo didn't stop to think, though in truth, she wouldn't have done anything differently if she had. She ran at the man, landing a punch to his nose that wouldn't have done nearly as much damage if she hadn't had a running start and all her weight behind it.

As it was, beer paunch landed on his fat kid-shaking ass.

"You broke my goddamned nose, you bitch!" he yelled through the blood blooming behind the hands he was holding to his face.

Mo landed in the back of a Justus Police cruiser.

"I'm not doubting you, Mo," Wade said, "But the kid's own mother was right there, and she's not willing to swear out a statement against her husband."

"And that lady's up for mother of the year. That's who you ought to be arresting. Just for being a piece of work."

"Lydia Gresham's got her own crosses to bear."

Wade held up a hand when she opened her mouth to tell him what she thought about Lydia Gresham and her crosses.

"Enough. I'm not saying it's right. But you're not the one going home with Lou tonight, battered, bloody, and humiliated in front of half the town. I don't know that you have any idea what kind of purgatory that woman lives in. And you didn't make it any better."

"And what was I supposed to do, Wade? Let him toss Tate around like a rag doll?"

"No. I can't imagine you doing anything different than you did, Mo. But you've got to understand there are consequences—"

He threw up his hands, realizing the futility of the lecture.

"Hell with it. You're free to go. You need a ride home?"

"That depends. Am I gonna have to sit in the back in handcuffs again?"

He rolled his eyes.

"Come on, Mabry. Let's get out of here."

Wade gave her a lift back to Red Poppy. He's grown up, Mo thought, almost against her will. It was late. The streets were quiet after the noise of the fairgrounds.

"Mo, I'm no expert on parenting," he said, breaking the silence. "But I do know that Tate is better off away from Lou. Hell, most people are better off away from Lou."

He glanced over at her.

"For all her faults, Lydia got the boy out of there."

Nobody's going to be pinning a medal on the woman's chest any time soon, Mo thought, but she held her tongue, turning her head to watch the night go by.

When they pulled up the drive, there were still a few lights on but not many.

"About that favor," he said, putting the SUV into park. Mo had nearly forgotten about the information she'd asked Wade to track down for her earlier that afternoon. He reached into the console and handed her a folded slip of paper.

"I found what you're looking for."

Wonder at what she held in her hand made Mo reckless. She leaned over and planted a kiss on Wade before she had time to consider it. It was an uncomplicated kiss, with no promises and no expectations.

At least she hoped it was.

She gave him a grin when they broke apart.

"You're a good guy, Ashbrook," she said, opening the door to step out.

"Am I? I better tuck that away. I must be slipping."

Mo was still smiling when the cruiser pulled down the

drive.

"Brought home by the police again?"

Mo glanced up in surprise, her smile fading as she realized she wasn't alone. Her aunt's bed had been wheeled out to the side porch that connected to her room by big French doors. She lay there, bathed in yellow porch light and shadows.

Maybe she just wanted some air, but more likely she'd asked Iona to move her out here to wait for her niece.

"What do you want?" Mo said.

"Tate's impressed with you. Sadie too, but Tate's the hard nut to crack."

Mo looked at the woman, who looked down upon Mo from her vantage point above the driveway.

"I'm not staying here."

"They need you."

"Do they? Do they really? Or do you need to control everything around you? Manipulate it like a you're some sort of wizard?"

Roz had always had a hard stare, but now that it was one of the few weapons left to her, it had been whittled down to concentrated flint.

"Go on then. Get out of here, if that's what you want so badly. But you'll go empty handed."

Mo let out a short laugh.

"Like that's anything new."

"Maybe not, but this time I have something you want."

"Arlo was right. Someone *should* put you down."

"You'd still be empty handed. And it's going to stay that way until I think you're ready."

"Ready for what?"

"Ready to handle the truth you so badly want."

Mo shook her head.

"Roz, it's late. So you can perch up there like a fat spider, spinning your web all you want, but I'm tired of listening to it."

She walked off, leaving Roz to stare at the darkness.

Mo was exhausted. She had little left to give, but she knew the night wasn't ready to let her rest. Walking into the quiet house, she got a beer from the kitchen and headed back to the front porch.

Thankfully, she couldn't see or hear her aunt from there. The similarities between the two of them played an unfriendly game of hide and seek in the corner of her mind, but she ignored that and leaned back in the porch swing, propping her feet on a stool.

She listened to the sounds around her. The darkness was full of life, as it so often is. And wasn't that the way of it. Life prevailed, under any conditions.

The beer was halfway gone when Mo's gaze fell on the beams that ran overhead. She set the bottle down and pulled the stool to the place she remembered. Feeling around above the thick beam, she found nothing at first. Then her hand made contact with the old cigar box.

She pulled it down, blowing the dust from the top.

Stepping down from the stool, she took the box back to her seat, and ran a hand over the faded red King Edward label. Lifting the thin cardboard lid, she saw some desiccated crumbles in the corner and one old dried-up joint.

Lifting it out, she was amazed it didn't disintegrate in her hands. She smelled the stale marijuana, and a ghost of a smile played at her lips.

"I asked Cal about you," Tate said from the shadows. "About what you were like when you were younger."

"Yeah?" A sad sort of calm had settled on her, and she found herself glad for his company.

"But I don't believe him."

"You don't, huh."

"Nobody'd be dumb enough to steal a cop car and run it out on that rusty old train trestle. Not even you."

Mo set the joint back in the box and closed the lid.

"That old piece of junk wouldn't hold no car."

"Not for long it wouldn't. That much I can say for certain."

Tate gawped at her.

"I thought Cal was messing with me."

Mo raised her beer to her lips.

"It must be forty, fifty feet up."

"Probably so."

Mo stared out into the darkness. She could still remember the unadulterated joy of realizing the couple she and Phil had spotted going into the shacks from their perch on the trestle bridge included the Chief of Police and an unidentified woman that no one figured was his wife.

"No freaking way," Phil had said, his mouth hanging open.

"Come on, I have an idea," Mo'd told him, as she rose and began making her way across the bridge. Phil had followed along, always willing to get her back. In a purely selfish way, it was her favorite thing about him.

They'd found the chief's car parked along the road, lights dark and trying to hide, tucked into some brush. Mo didn't know who he thought he was fooling. It was like trying to hide an elephant in a berry patch. A black and white elephant with a police emblem on the side. She guessed he was too caught up in the excitement of his illicit date to be thinking more clearly.

"It's not like he's gonna leave the keys in the ignition," Phil had whispered.

But that didn't matter. One of Della's boyfriends had taught her how to hot-wire a car when she was ten. She'd liked that guy. He was the one who'd taught her to play pool, too.

It only took a few minutes, and the car came to life beneath them.

"Holy shitballs," Phil breathed from the front passenger seat, and she knew by the look on his face that he felt as alive as she did in this moment.

"I didn't know you could do that."

Mo hadn't been sure herself, but her hands had remembered what to do.

Luckily, the shacks were too far away for the couple to hear the sound of the engine as it purred. And they were busy with other deeds.

When Mo backed the car onto the road, keeping the lights dark, and shifted into drive, she reveled in the feeling of unhinged power that surged through her. Any feelings at all had been hard to come by the last few years, but this one was here. She was going to squeeze it for every drop.

Phil yelled to some chaotic god as they took off down the street, and Mo grinned.

There's a reason they call it joyriding. But every joy fades. Mo tried hard to hold onto it, but it eventually slipped through her fingers, all the same.

After a time, she turned the car back toward the river.

"Where are you going? You're not gonna just take it back, are you?"

"That's exactly what I'm gonna do," she said. "Sort of."

When Mo turned the car into the woods along the forgotten track where the trains used to travel, Phillip went along. As they followed the tracks, long overgrown, the car pushed the brush out of the way in front of them. And still Phillip went along.

When she stopped the car just before the ground fell away below the tracks, with the old bridge laid out against the moonlit night, Phil still didn't waver.

"Are we leaving it here?" he'd asked.

"No," she said. "We're leaving it there." Mo nodded toward the bridge.

And Phil balked.

"You're crazy," he said, staring at her like he was seeing her for the first time. "You got a death wish."

She didn't. She didn't have any wish at all. Except to chase away the yawning cavern of numb she'd been existing in.

Phillip had clambered out of the car, slamming the door behind him, all thoughts of secrecy gone.

When Mo pulled the car slowly onto the tracks, with the

wheels bumping along the slats, she could feel again. The further from the banks of the river she got, the sharper and more exciting those feelings became.

When she reached the middle of the bridge, she stopped the car. Stepping carefully out of the driver's side door, she could see the river winking at her in the moonlight below. She knew she'd never get this back.

She'd planned to leave the car there, a parting shot at a feckless authority. But she couldn't bear to fade into nothing again. Instead of walking slowly along the precarious tracks back to the river's edge, as she should have, Mo walked to the front of the car.

She slid onto the hood, the engine still warm and ticking. Then she made her way forward, climbing onto the roof of the car.

Mo had stood there, on the top of the stolen cruiser, in a place that had long since rusted past the point of usefulness and she stared at the river moving below. At the strength and implacability she saw there.

She thought maybe this was where she belonged. Rivers don't feel anything either.

When the world around her decided to up the stakes and the trestle started to creak and shift, Mo had no cards left to play.

As the planks the car was balancing on gave way and the cruiser below her started to buck and tilt, she knew it was going into the water. So Mo did the only thing left to do.

She flew.

"I heard what you said to Roz," Tate said, pulling her back from her memory. "About not staying."

She glanced at the boy's face, but he was staring off into the night.

"Look, kid…"

"No, it's cool. I understand. Just do me a favor. Don't bullshit me, okay."

Tate stood and walked quietly back into the house.

Mo ached for him.

She reached into the forgotten cigar box and pulled out the joint. With an old box of matches, that shouldn't by all rights light, she lit the joint. Without bothering to bring it to her lips, she watched it burn.

For as long as Mo could recall, her aunt had run a business selling small-batch, handmade soaps and lotions and creams. They had ingredients like lemon verbena and lavender. Aloe and calendula. Many of those, Roz grew in her gardens here at Red Poppy.

When Mo was younger, Roz had sold locally, using her old green international truck to deliver the bottles and pots with their vintage labels to shops and stores ranging over several counties. Apparently, she still did. At least, she had up until she'd been incapacitated. In addition, the world wide web had made its way to even a backwater like this.

"Roz has orders backing up. Sadie and Tate are going to help me update her stock and get those orders shipped out today," Georgia had told Mo that morning.

With an eyebrow up, Mo didn't ask how her friend knew this.

"Okay then. If that makes you happy."

And so she'd left them, collecting herbs and poring over handwritten recipe books that had been in the Mabry family for many generations.

Mo had somewhere to be.

Taking the jeep, she followed the map to the address Wade had given her. It took an hour and a half. Again, Mo felt that feeling that it should have been farther. That it *was* farther, in spite of the distance on the road.

Pulling into a trailer park two counties over, Mo had to shake off the sense of stepping back into time. She'd grown up in places like this. From the meanest ones full of junkies and half-naked children to the cleaner ones with hanging baskets of flowers, where the weeds were pulled and the community knew one another, Mo had seen them all. Most had been okay.

This one was closer to the bottom of the list.

She found lot number twelve. Next door there was an apathetic dog of indeterminate breed chained to a tree. The chain was unnecessary. The dog barely raised its head to glance her way when she stepped from the jeep. It lay panting in the dirt.

Taking the steps up to the front door of the trailer, Mo read the crooked sign nailed to the side of the door next to the back end of an air-conditioning window unit that dripped water into a muddy place below.

Psychic Readings, the faded sign read.

It was an old shtick. One Mo had seen many times in the past.

Trailers like this didn't have doorbells. Mo opened the aluminum screen door and knocked on the dimpled fiberglass front door behind it.

She could hear the thump of humanity moving about within. It was difficult to hide from the moths flapping about inside her brain, disturbed by her jaunt into the past.

When the door opened, a man stood there. An oddly shaped, oily sort of man. Age spots showed through his comb over.

Mo cleared her throat.

"I'm looking for Della," she said.

"I don't do readings until after two, honey. You'll need to come back then," said a voice from inside the shadows and the fake wood paneling within.

That voice. Mo swallowed. It had been a very long time.

The man must have assumed her business was done. He went to shut the door without even a fare-thee-well.

"I'm not here for a reading, Mama," Mo called.

The man stopped the door short, glancing over his shoulder with wide eyes.

There was a sound of a chair scraping on linoleum and a

shuffle of house shoes.

The woman who walked around the corner in a tatty house robe, with her hair up in old fashioned rollers, gave Mo vertigo. She was looking at a life-sized version of those cards they make for kids, the ones that change and move when you turn them this way and that.

At once, Mo could see the extra lines on her mother's face, the ones that had deepened along the corners of her eyes and the fine furrows dipping down into her lips. Yet, when she smiled and her cheeks filled out around those bright green eyes, Mo saw only the mother she'd always known, the one she'd come so far to come back to.

"Mimosa Jane," Della said wonderingly. "As I live and breathe. Get in here, child."

Della grabbed her in a hug. One Mo couldn't stop herself from falling into. She closed her eyes, overcome by the familiar scent of her mama. A combination of ivory soap, gardenia perfume and Virginia Slims. It hit Mo like a train.

"Oh, baby!" Della was saying, hugging her hard, then pulling back to look into her daughter's face.

"Oh, sweetheart, let me look at you. That red hair. You and that red hair, love. Like a red rose in bloom. I always knew you'd grow into a wild beauty." Della stroked Mo's head. The smile on her face was captivating. Mo couldn't look away.

"Otis, shut the door already. And pick up your chin, haven't you seen a woman and her daughter before?"

Otis did as he was told, a trait that had always been necessary in any boyfriend of Della's. At least, if they wanted to continue to be. Mo wondered how long this one had lasted.

"Don't mind him, honey. Come on in, I'll get you a drink. Otis, pull out that bottle of champagne I've been saving," she said, moving Mo with her into the trailer's tiny kitchen.

"Sit, sit," Della said. "I just can't believe you're here, Mimosa."

Her mother reached her across the chipped Formica table and took Mo's hands in her own. Her nails were a bright cherry red.

Mo could remember the two of them, painting their nails together. Della always with different shades of red.

Otis brought out a bottle of champagne and set it on the table with two mismatched mason jars.

"Otis, what are you doing? The good glasses," Della said.

He took the mason jars away and produced two crystal whiskey decanters.

He still hadn't said a word.

"Oh, Mimosa, honey. I had no idea when I woke up this morning I'd be seeing you today. I can't get over it. And me, I must look a sight." Della reached up to pat her hair down and realized she still had curlers there.

"Oh, my goodness, I've still got my rollers in!" She set to pulling out the pins, letting her blonde hair fall in a cap around her head. How many times had Mo watched her do just that? She couldn't count.

Della had aged, it was undeniable, but she still clung to the beauty of her youth. It was there, in the tilt of her head and the way she sat up straight, always, balancing an invisible book on her head.

"A lady can't show off her best features slumped in a chair, Mimosa," Della used to say.

"You should've called, honey, so I'd have known you were coming. I could've planned something special."

Mo didn't know her number, she thought, as she watched her mother pop the cork on a bottle of cheap champagne and pour them both a glass. She supposed Otis didn't rate one, as he'd disappeared into another room.

"I know what we need! We need to have a party! An impromptu get together and you can meet all my friends! Oh, Otis, honey, bring me my phone. We're gonna have us a party!"

Her mother had always taken life at such a frenetic pace.

Mo was used to it when she was younger, but now it made her head spin.

"Mama, Mama, slow down," she said, reaching across the table to take her mother's hand. The skin felt dry.

"Oh, but hon, we have to celebrate! But first, you've gotta tell me everything! How are you? What have you been doing with yourself? Oh, my, I should put some clothes on. Let me get decent, then I want to hear absolutely everything."

The speed at which the woman could pivot from one subject to the next was a marvel.

Mo watched her exit the room, feeling like a ship tossed on stormy seas.

"Roz is hurt, Mama," Mo said toward Della's bedroom. She rose from the table, leaving her whiskey glass of champagne untouched. She moved to the open doorway, trying to get a firmer grip on a situation that felt like it was slipping quickly from her control.

There was a pause. A moment when Mo wished she could see her mother's face; see how she took this news.

"Hurt?" Della said, coming out of the closet in her nylon nightgown, holding a dress on a hanger to her chest. "What do you mean, hurt?"

"She was attacked. She's been paralyzed."

There really wasn't a softer way to put it than that.

Della dropped onto the bed. It was difficult to read the emotions she saw flicker across her mother's face. Before she could get a hold of one, Della was on to the next.

"Is she... Is she gonna be okay? Is she going to live?" Della asked.

"Probably longer than any of us," Mo said. "But she's confined to a bed."

Della nodded slowly, taking it in.

"That's why I'm here, in a roundabout way. Not here, here, but here, at Red Poppy. Roz, well, Roz wanted me back. And she has something I want in return."

She was making a mess of this.

"I'm sorry, honey," Della said, shaking her head in

confusion. "I don't understand. Are you taking care of her?"

"Not exactly. Look, it's complicated and not really the reason I'm here. *Here* here, that is. With you."

Della looked at her, still for once. Mo couldn't stop the thought that her mother's beauty performed better when she was moving, vivacious. In rest, her age began to show.

"I'll let you get dressed. Then we'll talk."

Della nodded.

Retreating to the kitchen, Mo found a half pot of coffee that was still warm. Pouring herself a cup, she waited for her mother, something she was all too familiar with.

Finally, Della walked back into the room. Dressed and coiffed and in full make-up, she'd had time to pull herself together, both mentally and physically.

"Okay, now. You tell me what's going on, Mimosa."

Mo sighed.

"I don't even know where to start."

She filled her mother in as best she could on the state of things at Della's childhood home. She told her about Tate and Sadie. She told her about Emma and Georgia and Cal.

"But none of that's why I'm here. I need some answers, Mama."

Della looked at her with her head tilted to one side.

"Answers about what, hon?"

"What happened, all those years ago between you and Roz?"

It wasn't what Mo really wanted to know, but it was a fine enough place to start.

Della shook her head, looking away from her daughter's face.

"Oh, now, honey, that's all water under the bridge. We don't need to drag all that up again, now do we?"

"I think maybe we do."

"Why, it was all so long ago, I can't even hardly remember. Just sisters. Sisters never do see eye to eye."

"Was the room on the east side of the house, the one with the crib... Was that your room? Did we stay there, together?"

"Of course it was my room. That was my home too, you know. In spite of anything my sister did. It was my home, too."

Della rose. She was ruffled.

"Why did Roz throw us out? What happened?"

"I never did know," Della said, spitting out the words with a shake of her head. "Jealous, I suppose. That boy of hers, he was never going to amount to nothing. You could see that early on. And there I was, with you. She was jealous, and it ate her up."

"Is that all? Jealousy?" Mo knew it could be a powerful motivator, but it didn't sound like enough.

"Of course it is. Are you saying I'm lying?"

"No, Mama. I'm just asking if there's more to it than that. Arlo said something about secrets and—"

"Arlo Vaughn? That old huckster hadn't ever let a true word leave his mouth. Don't you listen to anything at all you hear from Arlo Vaughn. You hear me?"

Mo nodded, but her dissatisfaction couldn't be tamped down.

"But I still don't understand what happened. What happened later? Where were you?"

She'd finally circled around to the beating heart of the matter.

"Where were you when I needed you? Why did Roz come and take me away?"

Della wouldn't meet her eyes.

"Why did you let her?"

Her mother shook her head, backing away from questions that were too real to answer.

"Why are you doing all this Mimosa Jane? This is all in the past. Why in the world would you want to come here and drag all this up again?"

"Roz pulled me back here, Mama. It feels like she's holding me prisoner. Again."

"Well, that's ridiculous. You're grown, aren't you?"

"She knows something she's not telling me. Something I need to know."

Della stood, taking her whiskey glass to the sink and avoiding her daughter's eyes.

"She knows something about Lucy. Or she says she does."

Della turned and looked at her in frustration.

"Who's Lucy?" she asked, her irritation plain on every line in her face.

It was a knife to Mo's heart.

"My baby, Mama. Lucy was my baby."

Della managed to look embarrassed.

Mo's phone rang in her pocket. It was Georgia. Mo grabbed onto the call like a lifeline, needing to escape the pain she was drowning in.

"Hello," Mo answered as she stood from the table, turning her back on Della. She struggled to get a handle on the turmoil raging inside.

"Mo, you've got to get back here." Georgia was talking too fast, stumbling over her words.

"What's wrong?"

"It's Sadie, Mo. They've come for her, and they say there's nothing I can do and she's crying—"

"Wait, wait, who's come for her, Georgia?" Mo asked loudly over the noise in the background. She could hear Sadie begging someone, "Pleeeease!"

"They said they have to take her. Roz is trying to get them to talk to her, but they won't listen. And they're asking questions about Tate. Mo you have to come!"

"Georgia, *who*? Who is taking her?"

"CPS, Mo! They said she can't stay here, that she's a ward of the state—"

The screaming in the background grew louder.

"Stall them, Georgia, I'm on my way."

"Mo, I don't know how long I can—"

"Tell them to wait, by God! I'm coming!"

"But Mo—"

"Just do it! I'm on my way!"

Mo barely glanced at Della as she scooped up the keys to her jeep from the table.

"I've got to go, Mama," she said, running out the door.

Mo flew down the steps to the trailer, leaving the door swinging wide behind her.

When Mo pulled the jeep back into the drive at Red Poppy, she was frantic. The sounds of Sadie's screams had echoed in her head the whole way. Mo could only be grateful she hadn't passed any policemen as she'd barreled down the highway with her emergency flashers keeping time with her heart rate.

Miraculously, Georgia had managed to hold them off, but Mo took one look at the situation and knew it was too late. Sadie's time was up, and hers was too.

Sadie was in the back seat of a dark sedan, her head buried in her hands. There was a woman with a severe expression standing at the open door of the sedan, and she'd clearly run out of patience. Calvin was talking with her, gesturing angrily, but the woman's face was granite.

Mo ran up. The woman already had one foot in the damn car.

"Please, please wait. I'm here, can't we talk about this, can't we work something out?"

"Miss Mabry, I presume," the woman said, turning her hard gaze on Mo.

"Trust me when I say, Miss Mabry, that I have waited far longer than I should have. What you folks fail to accept is that there are laws. There are policies and procedures. And they're in place for a reason. Prolonging this event is serving no purpose other than traumatizing the child, and in spite of the fact that you believe me to be here for some nefarious purpose, I assure you, I do have that child's best interest at heart. That is my job. It's what I do. And if you want to help her, a sentiment I truly appreciate, by the way, I suggest you get out of my way and let me do my job. Now we are done here."

The agent stepped into the car and slammed the door, nearly taking out Mo's knee as she did.

Mo's eyed widened and she took a step back. This woman wasn't granite, she was steel. How Georgia and Calvin had managed to keep her here for so long, Mo had no idea.

Leaning out of her window, she glared at Mo.

"This child is a minor, not a pet. She's lost the only parent she's ever known, and the state has a responsibility to ensure that she's placed in an appropriate home. And rolling into town just long enough to say "Tag, I'm it," is *not* how things are done."

Mo placed a hand on the window to the back door of the car. Sadie looked up at her, her face filled with a sorrow Mo had never seen there before.

"You can't just take her!"

"I can," the woman said. "I should. And I am."

As the car rolled away, taking Sadie with it, Tate broke free of Georgia's arms and bolted off the porch, running after the car.

"Tate!" Calvin called, going after him.

Mo could only watch, unable to make it stop.

"Mo, oh God, Mo, I'm so sorry. We tried, I swear we tried everything we could think of."

Georgia's face mirrored Sadie's, from the red puffy eyes to the sadness that had taken hold there.

Mo hugged her friend while she cried.

The CPS agent was right, Mo knew. Of course, there were laws. Why that hadn't occurred to them sooner, she didn't know. It was a surreal side effect of living in this insular place, where Roz's word was rule.

Tate ran back to them, with Calvin on his heels.

"You have to get her back. This is her home. You don't

understand what it's like, you don't know—" Tate broke off, unable to hold back the sobs.

She leaned down on one knee in front of him.

"Shh," Mo said, pulling him to her.

For a moment, he clutched her with his skinny arms, then pushed her away.

"No!" he said. "I don't need a *hug*! I need you to get Sadie back!"

With that, he ran toward the house, leaving her kneeling in the dirt.

Seeing no other way, Mo followed him to the house, but she didn't seek out Tate in whatever corner he'd found to nurse his hurts.

He was right.

Walking into Roz's room, she got straight to the point.

"What do I do now? Help me fix this."

Her aunt must be railing at the sky inside, stuck as she was, a prisoner in her own home, in this bed, in her own worthless body. But she held it together.

"Get on the phone. Get Hayes over here. Now."

Mo could do nothing but pace.

Hayes had been holed up with Roz for over half an hour. She'd heard occasional shouting.

"…told you this was going to happen!"

"…not helping matters…"

"…have to tell her, by God…"

When the door was suddenly thrown open and the lawyer emerged, he looked like he'd gone ten rounds in the ring with a tiger.

"Talk to your aunt," he said, as he walked by, not pausing to chat. "She'll explain things. I have work to do."

And with that he was out the door.

Mo did as he suggested, not even letting the door to Roz's room swing shut behind him.

"Well?" She could hardly dare to hope they'd come up with a solution.

"Hayes is going to start the process of making this a legitimate foster home, in the eyes of the state of Texas."

"Will that work? How long will it take?"

"It'll take some time. There are procedures."

"Procedures that you've taken it upon yourself to ignore up until this point!" Mo said, throwing up her hands.

"Well?" she demanded, when Roz stayed silent.

"Go ahead and get it out, then. Blame me. You always do. When you're finished, I'll continue."

Mo wanted to argue. To fight and yell and scream. And she knew it would do absolutely no good.

"Fine," she said.

"Are you done?" Roz asked.

"Just tell me!"

Roz paused, presumably to see if Mo had anything else to add, then went on in a gratingly calm tone of voice.

"In the meantime, he's going to file a motion for temporary custody so that I can remain as Sadie's standby guardian while the courts decide what's best for her. That should be decided quickly, but a more permanent solution will take time. There are channels to go through, and there will have to be a search for the child's mother."

Sadie's junkie mother who felt like Nat Yates was the better option for her child. Outstanding.

"In the meantime, Mimosa, we need to talk about Tate."

Mo pulled the jeep slowly up the drive to the white farmhouse on the other side of town. The place was... well it was... pretty. Picturesque, even, nestled on a hill and bordered by a tall and wide-reaching stand of oaks.

It wasn't what she'd expected.

The grass was mown. The yard was free from the detritus that seemed to wash up along the shores of most of the homes around here. There were no rusted-out car remains, no dogs chained to trees. Instead, there were window boxes with petunias in them. There was an actual white picket fence, for Christ's sake.

It could have been a postcard. But like a postcard, she knew the image was as thin as the paper it was printed on.

The woman who answered the doorbell was as timid and mousy as Mo remembered.

Lydia Gresham gasped when she saw who her visitor was.

"You can't be here," she whispered, through a crack in the front door. "You've got to go."

Mo saw the move coming and managed to open the screen door and put a foot in, blocking the wooden front door behind it from slamming in her face.

"We need to talk," she said. "It's about Tate."

"Is he okay? Is he hurt? Oh God, what's happened?"

The woman raised her hand to her mouth, and Mo used the opportunity to push the front door wider and step inside.

"He's fine," she said.

Lydia let out a breath.

"Are you sure?"

Mo raised an eyebrow, not taken in by the motherly concern.

"Relatively sure, yes. Unless he's managed to stub his toe since I've been gone."

In spite of Mo's rudeness, Lydia didn't take the bait. And Mo really wanted her to.

"Then I don't understand. Why are you here?"

"I'm here because the current situation can't continue."

Lydia looked more confused.

"What do you mean? Has he done something to make Ms. Mabry mad? If he's done something, I'm sure he didn't mean anything by it. He's a good boy, really he is."

"Yes, I know," Mo said pointedly. "The problem isn't with Tate. It's with you."

"Me? If I've offended Rosalind somehow, please, can

you tell her how sorry I am?"

Lydia looked so frightened, so apologetic, that Mo actually felt an unwanted stirring of sympathy sloshing around inside. She thought of what Wade had said about crosses to bear.

"No," she said, in a slightly gentler tone. "No, you haven't done anything. And that's why I'm here."

"I'm sorry, I don't understand."

"Can we sit down and talk?"

Lydia looked around the spotlessly clean room they were standing in, looking as if she were trying to figure out where to stow her visitor so she wouldn't be seen.

"Where is your husband, Mrs. Gresham?"

"Lou," she said. "Lou's gone down to Cordelia to get a part for the tractor. But he'll be back for his lunch. You've got to be gone by then. You can't be here."

Mo had no desire to run into Lou again either, but the woman's cowed nature rankled. She glanced at her watch. It was only ten, they had some time.

"All right. I'll be long gone from here by the time Lou walks through that door. But we really do need to talk."

"Come in, then. I'll get us some coffee."

Mo followed Lydia to the kitchen, wondering why anyone bothered with a living room, when any living that counted got done in a kitchen or on a porch.

"I hope you don't mind if I finish up this pie while we talk. Lou wanted an apple pie with his supper tonight, and I've got to get them baked and set," Lydia said as she poured a cup of coffee for her uninvited guest.

Of course he did, Mo thought. Because you can't live in a Norman Rockwell painting without an apple pie cooling in the window. The bastard.

"No. No, that's fine. Don't let me stop you."

Lydia pulled some ice cold butter out of the freezer and set to cutting it with a fork into a bowl of flour. Mo didn't know that she'd ever actually seen anyone make homemade pie crust. For all her charm, Della wasn't exactly domestic and Roz wasn't the type either.

After a moment, Mo cleared her throat.

"We need to talk about Tate's situation."

Lydia glanced up, fear in her eyes.

"Ms. Mabry told me he could stay there as long as he needed to. Has she changed her mind?"

"Why don't you tell me about why he's there in the first place."

The woman's eyes dropped down to the work in front of her. She opened her mouth, then closed it again, not able to find the words.

"Is it Lou?"

Mo thought for a moment that she wasn't going to answer. Then quietly, she said, "I shouldn't speak against my husband. It's not Christian."

It wasn't Christian. Yeah.

"So you're telling me that Tate is better off with a quadriplegic in a hoarded house on the other side of town, than he is here. With his mother."

Lydia glanced up at her again.

"Ms. Mabry's always been real good to Tate," she murmured.

Deep down, Mo knew it was pointless to try and lead this woman off the path of servitude to Lou Gresham. She could see plainly, even before she'd said a word, that Lydia didn't have it in her to go against his wishes. Even for the sake of her son.

But that didn't mean Mo had to like it.

"Look, the arrangement you had with Roz has no weight behind it. CPS has come and taken the other child away. Roz is fighting to get her back, but we don't have any idea if it's gonna work or not."

"Sadie? They've taken Sadie? But why?"

"Her father died, and Roz never had legal guardianship. It's a mess, and Sadie's caught in the middle. We can't let that happen to Tate too."

"What are you saying?"

118

"I'm saying that if you want Tate to continue living at Red Poppy Ridge, then it's going to have to be done officially."

Mo reached into her bag and removed the large manila envelope that held the fate of one little boy inside.

"I was told that Lou is your second husband. That he's not Tate's biological father."

Lydia nodded, her eyes glued to the envelope like it might strike her.

"His father died when he was a baby. A drunk driver," she murmured.

"Lou took us in. He wasn't always this way."

Mo doubted that, but whatever.

"Mrs. Gresham, the way I see it, you have two choices. You can stand up to your husband."

Lydia shrank back into her seat, becoming smaller, if that was possible.

"Because Tate loves you. He will always love you. And he needs you. The only person who can take a stand for him is you."

The struggle in Lydia's eyes was evident.

"Or—you can sign these papers and give legal, permanent guardianship over to Roz."

"Permanent?" Lydia looked panicked, near tears.

"But this is only temporary," she murmured. "I always thought, after a while, when he was a little older and Lou…"

Temporary? It had been two years.

"I know what *I* believe. I believe he'd be better off with you, his mother."

"I love Tate! I love my boy, I do."

Tears started to leak from Lydia's eyes. Even her tears were timid.

"I'm not saying you don't. I am saying it doesn't matter what I believe. Or Lou. You are Tate's legal guardian, and it's your signature that's needed on this paperwork."

Mo slid the envelope across the table.

"Wash this cup, then put it away," she told the broken

woman as she stood. "You don't want Lou to know anyone was here."

Mo had made it all the way to the front door before Lydia spoke again.

"I do love my son, Miss Mabry," she said.

But there was no heft to her words.

With her hand on the door knob, Mo spoke.

"Then bring him home to you. Or sign those papers. I can't make that decision for you."

And with that, she left Lydia Gresham standing in her beautifully clean kitchen, wringing her hands on a towel and looking like the world was crushing her beneath its weight.

And Mo supposed it was.

Mo had never understood the affinity southerners had for abandoning their fully air conditioned kitchens to sit out in the heat and the all-consuming humidity, fighting off the bugs, to cook meat under open flames.

And yet, there she was, watching Calvin burn rib-eyes and hot dogs in the yard while she kept to the shade of the porch, hiding from the late afternoon sun.

Wade was there too, sitting next to her, out of uniform today. A day off looked good on him, she thought. And the companionable silence, as they sipped cold beer, was good for her.

"You're burning those steaks, you old goat," Georgia called from the door.

"Get back into the kitchen, woman. Meat and fire are man territory," Cal yelled back.

"I'll show you man territory. Don't you burn my steak, Calvin Mabry. I told you I like mine medium-rare."

"Just you hush up. Old goat, my ass," he said. The flames licked up on a slab of meat in front of him that was way past medium rare, pulling his attention away from the blonde standing in his doorway.

"Tate, go grab me a plate, son," Calvin called. Tate was petting the kittens on the porch. He was quiet today, without his sidekick, but he did as he was asked.

The hole left by the missing Sadie was an open wound in their midst.

Mo tried hard to console herself with the thought that they were doing what they could. They *would* bring her back. Hayes would make it happen. But that didn't stop her from wondering what Sadie was doing now, if she was safe, if she was sad.

"Next time, I'm cooking the steaks," Georgia said, dropping down next to Wade and Mo.

Mo looked at her friend. There was still a shadow, there in her face, one that hadn't left since Sadie had been taken. But there was more there, too.

"You're settling in," Mo said.

Georgia looked over at Calvin, who was fumbling one of the steaks. He managed to catch it before it landed in the dirt. There was a small smile on her face.

"I'm not like you, Mo," she said quietly. "I don't have anything to prove. Not to myself and not to anyone else. I'm going to stay here and accept, graciously I hope, what fate has handed me."

Georgia rose and leaned over to press her lips to Mo's cheek, then took a cold beer to Cal. The smile he gave her was full of a lot of things Mo had never known.

Her words had stung a little, but she found she was happy for her friend. Happy for them both.

"Do you think she's right? Do you think I have something to prove?" Mo asked Wade.

"Hmm?" he asked, suddenly very interested in the weathered wood of the porch.

"Don't pretend like you didn't hear me."

He looked up and met her eyes, his face serious.

"You really want to know what I think?"

"I asked, didn't I."

He thought for a moment, then shook his head.

"I think you're fighting a lot of battles. On all fronts. You always have. No way around that. But I do wonder..."

He broke off.

"What? Spit it out, then."

"I wonder if you'll know how to be, once the war is over. If you'll even recognize when it is."

"That's not fair," she said quietly.

Wade sighed.

"My granddad used to tell me, Wade, buddy, fair is where you sell your pigs."

"Charming," she said, lifting a brow in his direction.

Everyone looked up when they heard the crunch of gravel under tires. There was a car coming up the drive.

Mo stood, thinking just once, she'd like to see a car show up bringing some good news. Was it too much to ask?

As Lydia stiffly got out of the driver's side, Mo could see by her demeanor that it wouldn't be today.

Mo walked to the car to meet her. The cakey layer of make-up Lydia was wearing did little to brighten her face, but Mo could tell she hadn't applied it so heavily to highlight her features. It did a poor job of masking the bruises she'd tried so hard to cover up.

What is it with men and their fists, Mo wondered.

Lydia had the manila envelope in her hand. Mo was reminded of the chained up dog next to her mother's trailer.

She handed the envelope to Mo.

"I tried... I did," Lydia whispered. "Don't think badly of me."

"Mama," Tate cried from the house, taking the steps two at a time and coming down to meet them. For that moment, he had the face of the innocent eleven-year-old boy he should have been.

"It's not my opinion that counts, lady," Mo told her under her breath.

She saw the way Lydia winced when Tate hit her with the running embrace, even as she hugged him back.

"Are you here to take me home?" he asked, before he

got a good look at his mother's face. When he looked up, Mo could see his expression change.

"No, honey, not yet. Not yet. I just wanted to say hi. I know I missed your birthday, so I brought you something," she said, counting on the distraction to placate a boy who was wise beyond his years.

Lydia moved to the back door of the car, opening it to retrieve what she'd brought for her son. Mo watched him closely. Tate's face was a mask of wax as he took in how slowly his mother moved, favoring her right side as she was.

She pulled out a new leather baseball glove wrapped in a blue ribbon, tied in a bow.

Lydia knelt down to hand it to him, then grasped him in a hug. Mo could still see Tate's face, devoid of any emotion as his eyes fell on the envelope Mo was holding in her hand. He didn't meet Mo's eyes.

When his mother leaned back and looked into the face of her son, searching his eyes for a forgiveness that she had no right to ask for, Tate forced a smile onto his face.

Mo had never seen anything so devastatingly sad.

"Are you doing okay here, Tate?"

He nodded his head and swallowed before he spoke.

"I love it here, Mama. It's great."

"I'm so glad, hon." Lydia smiled, though tepid tears were beginning to leak from her eyes, running tracks down her made-up face.

She gave him one more hug, then rose, trying to quickly dry her eyes around her false smile. She practically leapt back in the car.

"I love you, Tate, my beautiful boy. It's not forever. I'll be back for you when the time is right. One day. I will."

Mo could feel the choked-up sympathy that clogged her throat crystallize into anger at the lie.

"Okay, Mom," Tate said, with a smile on his lips and heartbreak in his eyes.

When Lydia drove away from her son, losing her fight against the tears as she went, Tate's smile and his new glove fell into the dirt.

"Tate—"

He waved a hand at her, cutting her off.

Without asking any questions or even looking her way, Tate ran off toward the direction of the river.

Mo took a step to follow him, but Calvin stopped her.

"Let him go, Mimosa."

So she let him go.

"He knew she was lying," Mo said.

"Yeah."

"How could she?" she asked, her voice rising.

"How could she what?"

"How could she be so... so *weak*?"

Her uncle shook his head.

"Mo, being weak isn't hard."

"He should be with his mother."

Calvin leaned down to pick up the leather glove. The blue ribbon was dusty and coming loose. He held it out to her.

"Are you sure about that?"

Unbidden, there was a sound in her head, as hollow and empty as the day she'd heard it. The sound of the first handful of dirt falling onto Emma's casket, as she was put under the ground next to the mother she'd loved so completely.

Mo gave Tate some time and space, but when the darkness began to take hold around them and he still wasn't back, she followed the path he'd taken.

She took the glove with her, mostly so her hands would have something to hold.

When she got closer to the river, she saw him there, sobbing like he'd never stop hurting again. Mo knew there were no words that could take away that kind of hurt. The kind that tore through you in a deep down place.

Carefully, she leaned down and left the glove in the path so he'd find it when he came back.

He would want it.

Or he wouldn't.

That was up to him.

Making her way back to the house, Mo could feel herself coming untethered. Rather than lose it in front of the others, she found a pine tree to lean her back against and took a long, deep breath, but it did little good.

The raw emotion, the thorny mass of hurt that was coming off of Tate had scraped its way past her, dislodging a scab that had been giving way for days.

Leaning her head onto her knees, Mo's abdomen clenched at the memory of the labor pains. At the all-consuming need she'd had for her mother.

She'd cried, between the contractions that had grown closer and closer together, calling out for her, begging Iona and Roz to bring her a phone, or call Della themselves.

"She said she'd be here," Mo had screamed. "She promised she'd be here. I need her here!"

"Enough already!" Roz had finally said. "Your mother's been called Mimosa. Against my wishes, I might add."

Mo had seen the look that passed between her aunt and the nurse, who'd been with them, unspeaking, for hours.

"She's been called. She was already here. I sent her away. I won't have her in my house."

And with that proclamation ringing in her ears, a tearing contraction had ripped through Mo. She'd screamed, her body forcing her to push whether she was ready or not. And with hatred for her aunt coursing through her, Mo had brought her daughter into the world.

Mo tossed the manila envelope on the top of the dresser in her aunt's room.

"You did it. You got what you wanted. Lydia Gresham

turned over guardianship of Tate to you."

If she'd been expecting a word of thanks, or even a smile, she'd have a long wait.

"No, she didn't," Roz said.

"Why do you always have to be this way? She did. There's your paperwork, signed and sealed. It's done."

Roz said nothing. Only watched her niece in the silence that stacked up around them. Watched and waited.

"What's going on, Roz?" Mo asked suspiciously.

But her aunt gave nothing away with her stare.

Mo's pulse started to race. She sensed there was danger here, hiding in the middle of the room. Something she'd yet to see.

Finally, Mo reached for the envelope. She stared back at her aunt as she put a finger under the flap to rip it open. When her gaze dropped to the papers in her hand, she scanned them. They were, in fact, guardianship documents. Her eyes fell further down the page.

And there it was.

Lydia Gresham hadn't handed her son over to Roz.

No.

She'd given him to her.

Mo stared down at the second name on the page, below an empty signature line. Mimosa Jane Mabry, it said. Right there, in black and white.

"What have you done?" Mo whispered.

"It's up to you now. Sign those papers and you're officially responsible for that boy."

Mo tried to get a handle on her anger, but the blood pounding in her ears made it difficult to comprehend what was right in front of her. She couldn't speak. She was afraid she was very close to coming apart at the seams.

"What did you think, Mimosa? That I could continue to care for these kids? I'm a quadriplegic, for God's sake."

"Sadie?" Mo said, deliberately keeping her voice soft. She knew if she started to scream, she'd never be able to stop.

"No court will grant custody of a six-year-old girl,

temporary or otherwise, to a woman who can't even wipe her own behind, you little fool."

"But Hayes... He said—"

"Exactly what I told him to. He's filed for temporary emergency custody for *you*, Mimosa. Not me."

"But I didn't sign anything!"

Roz shook her head at her niece.

"Do you really think I'd let something like a signature stop me?"

"I didn't want this! I didn't ask for this!"

Roz let out a short, humorless laugh.

"Do you think anyone ever does? Do you think I asked for this? Since when has what a person *wants* ever mattered?"

"You can't do this to me," Mo said, as she backed away from the cobra in the bed. "I'm not gonna let you do this to me."

Roz's gaze grew colder, if that was possible.

"You're right. I can't. The choice is yours. To step up, or to walk away and never look back. Leave Sadie to the system. Leave Tate to the whims of his horror of a stepfather."

Roz looked away from her.

"Do it then. If you can. If you think you'll be able to sleep at night. I wish you the best."

"You have never once, in my entire life, wished me the best!"

Roz sighed.

"Haven't you learned anything, Mimosa? Sometimes a lie is the only bridge across a great gaping chasm of the truth."

Garbage. It was all garbage, rolling out of her mouth, rotten and stinking.

"That's a pretty image, Roz. One you obviously believe. But it's not real. It's not *real*. And if it's not real, then what good is it?"

"You should know, child. You've turned into a master of ignoring what's right in front of your face."

"What's that supposed to mean?"

Mo was losing it. If she stayed in this room any longer, she was going to do grave physical harm the woman in front of her.

Roz sighed again and looked away.

"Nothing," she said. "Nothing at all. I'm an old woman, Mimosa, and I'm tired. Do what you want. I can't stop you."

PART IV

THE LAST SUPPER

Mo found herself wandering by the river again, the darkness blanketing her turmoil and confusion.

She'd never found serenity in religion, like she knew so many others did. It sounded too good to be true, to a cynical soul. But here, by the river, she found the closest thing to spirituality, to contentment, she'd ever come across. She wanted that now, needed it desperately.

Was this place really where she wanted to stay? By the river, she could come within sight of seeing it as a possibility. But the thought of the red house that stood behind her and the woman who lived within it—blanketing the place with deceit, like blood spatters at a crime scene—made her skin crawl.

It was too much. Too much to ask when her walls had already been weakened from inside, with the past pushing and grinding its way into her present.

Mo couldn't fight against all sides. The pain was ready, waiting there as it always had been. Waiting for her to acknowledge it, to face it, after all this time. She didn't know if she was ready. Didn't know if she'd ever be ready.

She gave up. The floodgates broke, washing her away in the memories of the past, where the horrible pressing, ripping sensation that was childbirth took all sense of will out of her hands and took on a life of its own.

The stone-faced nurse was there, at the bend in her knees. Roz was in a chair by her side. Not for comfort, neither of them, but to witness. There was no hand holding. No caressing of foreheads, only Mo's anger and Roz's stalwart and hated presence.

With a final scream that pulled the veins from her throat and a push that felt like everything inside of her was coming out, her part was done. She could breathe.

There was a flurry of activity as the baton was passed to others, and all attention turned from her, leaving her bleeding and in the dust.

But something was wrong.

It was clear even on the faces of the two hard women in the room with her.

Something was very wrong.

Iona was doing something, something desperate, to her baby. Mo struggled to see her hands, but the woman's back was to her, as she dipped low then pulled up again. Time was passing. So very much time.

For years afterward, perhaps forever afterward, the sound of a baby crying would have a visceral effect on her. Because that was the sound she'd expected, that she'd needed to hear. It was the sound that she never got.

There was no sound at all, except for the sound of a sink hole opening up inside of her.

Her own voice echoed down its cavernous depths.

"Give me my baby."

But the two women had ignored her as if she weren't even there, focused on the bloody bundle between them.

"A doctor?" Mo heard her aunt ask Iona, and true and complete panic blossomed in her breast.

"Give me my baby!" she screamed.

"Mimosa, not now," her aunt said, as if she were a spoiled preschooler demanding a treat.

Iona shook her head.

"It's too late for that."

And Mimosa lost her mind, struggling to get out of the bed.

"Give me my baby! Give me my baby, damn you! She's mine! Give her to me!"

Rosalind pushed her back into the bed and held her down as she fought against her aunt.

In the furthest, darkest corner of her mind, unspoken and unacknowledged, there was a brutal truth. That she needed this child, needed it to cling to as both an anchor and a savior. Her lifeline. Her reason for bothering to stay alive.

And it wasn't to be.

Iona laid the child down upon a dresser, and from somewhere there came a syringe.

Her aunt held her down as she screamed, unintelligible sounds that came from her core, as she was no longer able to put her pain into words. Roz held her as the nurse pushed the needle into her arm.

And all was black.

For the first time in a great many years, Mo felt the burning pressure of tears building behind her eyes. She sucked in a breath, then caught it there, hoping to push the tears back down. She thought if she started crying now, she might break, utterly and completely.

And that was how Tate found her, sucking in breaths that she swallowed, desperately hoping the air here, by the river, could dilute her hurt.

When she saw him standing there, so small with his skinny arms, she saw a fellow shipwreck survivor, washed up on this shore with her.

At least she wasn't alone. There was a small amount of comfort in that.

"You okay?" he asked.

She opened her mouth, and a near hysterical snort came out.

"No, I'm not, since you ask."

He sat down next to her.

"Want to talk about it?"

She didn't. Not really. Not really at all.

But as she looked at this kid with his sincerity, which should have, by all rights, been burned away by now, with his eyes puffy and red, she heard the words come out of her mouth.

"I have trouble sometimes, being able to see the line between truth and lies," she said slowly. "When I was a kid, not much older than you, people started lying to me. Hell, maybe even before that. And they've never really stopped."

"You mean Roz?"

She nodded.

"Big lies?"

She sighed.

"Yeah. You could say that."

He nodded sadly.

"I guess you know all about that," she said.

"Yeah. You could say that."

In the silence that followed, Mo came very close to telling Tate the truth about his own fate and how tenuous it was at the moment.

She wouldn't lie to him, but she hadn't made any decisions about their now inextricably entwined fates. And regardless of what pithy thing Wade's granddad might have to say about it, it wouldn't be fair to extend the possibility to Tate, only to yank it back again.

So did that mean Roz had turned her into a liar now, too?

The answer to that sat heavy on Mo's shoulders, squeezing in next to other ugly things squatting there.

Another restless night found Mo watching the clock tick-tock by in the early hours of the morning. Impatient, she finally picked up the phone and dialed Hayes' number, well before a decent time.

"What were you thinking letting Roz con you into

putting my name on anything, you old bastard? You, of all people, ought to know better. But I guess that's what you do, isn't it? When she says *froggy*, you say *how hi, ma'am?*"

"Mimosa," came the resigned reply. She'd woken him up and found the meanest of pleasures in that. But it wasn't enough.

"Are you even a real lawyer, Hayes? Where did you get your law degree, exactly? The taco stand next door to Yale?"

Whatever he said after that was muffled, but Mo didn't care.

"I want to know what you're going to do about the mess you've helped to make here, Hayes. And I want to know right now."

"Mimosa—"

"Don't you placate me, you son of a bitch. You're sliding fast down a steep hill heading nowhere good, and I'm not about to let you take me down with you."

"Come by my office later," he said, in a tone that implied he'd had a long string of very bad days, and this one wasn't shaping up to be any better.

"We have a lot to talk about."

Did he think he was being funny?

"You believe we have a lot to talk about, you—"

Mo stopped short and turned at the sound of the doorbell. Her mouth dropped open as she stared at the door like it was playing tricks, daring it to do it again.

The sun hadn't fully risen in the sky. Who would be ringing the doorbell at such a godforsaken hour?

Without a word of farewell to Hayes, Mo ended the call.

When she opened the door, Mo couldn't have been more shocked.

There stood Della, in full make-up and decked out in her best dress and heels. The smile on her face shimmered like a desert illusion. With the sun rising behind her, Mo would have been hard pressed to tell you which was brighter. Also behind Della, there was Otis, looking much the same, and no better, as the last time Mo'd seen him.

"Mama?" Mo said.

"Well, don't leave me standing on the doorstep, honey. Invite me in. The prodigal has returned."

With that, she swept past her daughter, with Mo, Otis, and several cases of luggage trailing in her wake.

The day that passed was surreal. Mo kept glancing at her mother, seeing her here in this house, and it would give her the smallest of jolts. She'd lose track of what she was doing or saying mid-stride and have to give herself a shake.

It was like seeing your long lost first crush on the way to your wedding. Or your Sunday school teacher living under a bridge. It was difficult to assimilate.

The one person who didn't seem to feel any awkwardness in the situation was Della herself. Of course, she'd grown up here. To her, this was her family home and always would be.

And she proceeded to settle in.

Tate, Calvin and Otis were conscripted to carry luggage and rearrange furniture as Della saw fit.

One might have expected her to settle into her old room, but no.

"Oh, no, Mimosa, love, this room is much too small. And this house has so very many to choose from."

"Most of them are full, Mama," Mo said.

"Well, why don't we take a look around and see for ourselves. I'm sure we can do better than this."

The place wasn't exactly the Four Seasons, and there were only so many rooms to choose from.

"Oh, now this is more like it," Della said, when she opened the door to the bedroom her parents had shared when they were alive.

Mo raised an eyebrow. She herself wouldn't feel particularly comfortable at the idea of sleeping in the bed where she'd potentially been conceived, but Della didn't seem bothered in the least.

"Oh, yes, this'll do just fine. Otis, honey, bring those bags up the stairs and put them in here, will you."

Mo was sent to track down clean sheets, and Della and Georgia set to dusting. After a few moments, Della's allergies began to act up, and after a few ladylike sneezes, she excused herself to the front porch to have a glass of tea and get some fresh air. Mo helped Georgia finish getting the room ready.

"So that's your Mom," Della said. "She's... different than I expected."

"Different than me, you mean?" Mo said with half a smile.

"Well... yeah."

"When I was little, I used to think there was something wrong with me," Mo said.

"There is."

"Funny. That's funny."

"But true."

"I thought Mama had a special radio that played in her head, songs that only she could hear. She danced through her days. Through her life. And I didn't have one."

Mo gave a sad smile at the bittersweet memory of those days and years when it'd been just her and a mother with songs in her head.

"It wasn't until I got older that I realized most people were like me. That Della was the one who was different. The one who was special."

Mo glanced at her friend and caught the look of sadness there, for the briefest of moments. Then Georgia smiled.

"Don't sell yourself short, Mo. You're halfway to crazy now. It's not a big leap to hearing voices in your head. You've still got time."

She threw Mo a wink and went back to cleaning the windows.

But Georgia was right about one thing. She and Della *were* different. If the women of the Mabry family were lined up one next to the other, Mo knew who would pass for mother and daughter, on the strength of unpleasantness alone.

Della was the one who was different.

Dinner that evening felt as strange as the day that came before it. There were no steaks on the grill in the yard, no frozen pizza tonight.

Della wanted to celebrate her homecoming.

After a morning spent compiling a list, she'd sent Calvin and Tate off to the grocery store. When they returned, to Mo's surprise Della had found an apron in the kitchen and proceeded to produce a meal the likes of which Mo had rarely seen.

There was chicken roasting with vegetables and herbs in the oven. Asparagus, a green salad, corn on the cob, drenched in butter. In a day marked by firsts, it may have been the most difficult thing for Mo to wrap her head around.

This was a far cry from the microwave chicken nuggets and boxed macaroni and cheese she'd grown up on.

"Where'd you learn to do this, Mama?" Mo asked from the barstool where Della had set her to work slicing tomatoes for the salad. ·

"From Manfred, of course," Della said, glancing at her daughter in surprise. "You remember Manfred. The chef."

"No, Mama. I never met Manfred."

"Of course you did. Short man, stocky, with lady lips."

"No."

"Oh. Well. I suppose that must have been after your time," Della said, waving her hand and going back to wrapping prosciutto around the asparagus spears. Where the guys had managed to procure prosciutto in Justus was a mystery.

"Manfred was something else," Della smiled at her. "He was a man with big appetites. Big appetites for *everything* life has to offer. Drinking, dancing, food. Unfortunately, those appetites extended to other women. But oh, we had a fine time while it lasted."

Mo tried to smile, but her mouth felt heavier than it had before.

"Have you spoken to Roz yet, Mama?"

Mo was sure her aunt knew her younger sister had arrived on her doorstep. There was little that got past her and the ever-present eyes of Iona.

"Oh, I think tomorrow's soon enough for that. I'll go and see her tomorrow. I just have to work up the courage, love. We didn't exactly part on the best of terms. But I do hope I can mend that. That's why I'm here, after all."

"Is it? Is that why you're here?"

"Well of course, Mimosa. Why else? Now why don't you go set the dining room table for me. And none of those chipped everyday plates. My grandmother had a fine set of china. I'm sure it's still here somewhere."

Mo did as she was told.

By the time Della called them all to dinner, the dining room looked like it belonged in another era. A throwback to the days of the ferryman's wife, maybe.

Candles flickered on the long table, set with pretty white china and real linens. There were silver utensils that had appeared and been brought back to a glorious shine. There were even bouquets of wildflowers picked from outside and placed in vases.

And Della reigned over it all, the benevolent hostess welcoming them to her table.

"Calvin, can you carve the chicken for us, love?" Della asked her brother.

Calvin had been particularly quiet since the arrival of his younger sister. Not unhappy to see her, exactly, but Mo had to wonder what was going through his head.

Tate was more open about his views.

"This is weird," he'd whispered to her as they sat down to dinner.

Mo opened her mouth to say something that might put him at ease. Nothing came to mind.

"Yeah. Yeah, it is."

Della was the only one of them who seemed absolutely and completely at home. For the rest of them, the forced pleasantry was nothing more than smoke. Every last one of them knew there was another shoe still to drop.

A shoe that belonged to Roz.

"How long are you staying, Ms... I'm sorry, I'm not sure what I should call you," Georgia said.

"Oh, it's Mabry still. I never did marry, though I had a few close calls. But I never found a man worth his salt, for the long haul."

Mo glanced over at Otis, who was busy stuffing chicken in his mouth and looking down at his plate.

"No, I never slowed down long enough to hitch up my wagon. But you can call me Della, honey. Everybody does," Della said, patting Georgia on the hand.

Mo noticed she hadn't answered the question.

Like a specter rising from the grave, a figure materialized in the shadows of the doorway behind where Della sat at the head of the table.

"Well, isn't this fine," Roz said from a wheelchair Mo had never seen.

Iona stood silently behind her, the nurse's face giving away nothing at all.

Everyone turned. Della's debutante smile was frozen in place as she swung around to take her first look at the sister she'd been estranged from for most of their adult lives.

"I suppose I'll have to move my bedroom into the foyer if I expect anyone to bother to speak to me in my own house."

"Rosalind," Della breathed, a kid caught playing dress up in her mother's closet.

"Adelle," Roz said.

Her aunt was the only person Mo knew who used her mother's given name. And she so rarely spoke of her sister, it was like a fossil being unearthed to hear it said aloud.

"You're in my spot."

Iona moved Roz's wheelchair forward, forcing Della to stand, her chair scraping the floor behind her as she jumped back out of the way.

"Well, I don't believe that was necessary," Della mumbled, moving her chair around the corner of the table and crowding in next to Otis.

And just like that, Roz put an end to Della's reign as queen of the manor. Della now looked like what she was.

Uninvited.

It was scary and a bit awe-inspiring how quickly that had been managed.

"It's good to see you up and around, Roz," Calvin said calmly.

"This seems to be a special occasion," Roz said. "What are we celebrating?"

"My return, of course." Della's voice was chirpy. Too high.

Roz stared at her.

"I mean, given your condition, I thought..." Della's choo-choo train was losing steam.

"You thought what, exactly?"

Roz's eyes pinned her sister in place. If Della had somehow picked up the impression that being paralyzed would have softened Roz, she was mistaken. If anything, the woman had become harder, having been stripped of any semblance of warmth or compassion. The hardness was all that showed on her now. Crags and cliffs built of solid rock.

Yet Della persisted.

"I thought you'd need your family around you now, in your time of need. This whole business between the two of us, it's just silliness, Rosie. And it's long since time we let bygones be what they are."

Della waved a hand in the air, as if it were as easy as shooing away a fly.

"Is that what you believe? That it's all water under the

bridge?"

"Of course it is. It was all so long ago. And look around you. Can't you see how therapeutic it'll be, to be surrounded by your friends and loved ones in this trying time."

"Therapeutic? So it's my welfare you have in mind?"

Mo's eyes were riveted on her aunt. Della persisted, but it was clear to Mo that her entreaties were falling on deaf ears. She wondered why Della didn't see it and stop now. If this went much further, it was bound to get ugly.

"Who else's?" Della said, shaking her head. "Come on sis, let's bury the hatchet. It's time to stop living in the past. Look around you, everyone's happy and healthy and here to support you."

No one looked happy. Even Della's frothy façade was showing thin patches. And bringing up health had to be insulting to Roz, as she sat there unable to move, her head supported by padded wings on either side of her head. The awkwardness of witnessing this conversation was wafting through the room, settling around them all like a bad smell.

"Even Mimosa's come home to help!" Della said, gesturing at her daughter. "And look at her there, she's turned out fine. After everything's said and done, it was the right thing to do, sending her here."

Roz raised her eyebrows.

"Was it?"

"Wait, what?" Mo asked, breaking in on their little reunion.

"Why don't you ask Mimosa how she feels about that, Della. Now that she's an adult, perhaps she's found a different perspective on her previous stay here."

Della looked over at her daughter. She seemed to realize right away that she'd slipped, fallen into a trap. One Roz hadn't even needed to lay for her. It was one entirely of her own making.

"Oh, I don't think we need to drag all that back up again, do you?"

"Yes. Yes, I do," Mo said, watching her mother's face

closely.

"What did you mean *sending* her here? I wasn't sent here, Mama. I was taken here against my will."

Della looked around, glancing at Roz, but she found no ally there.

"Well, yes. Of course. I misspoke. Of course you were."

But a piece of the puzzle had fallen right out of her mother's mouth and landed on the table in front of Mo. It clicked too quickly and too tightly to be swept back under the rug again.

"Rosie, love, can we get you a plate?" Della said, attempting to derail the conversation that had jumped its tracks.

"I don't believe so, Adelle." Roz said quietly. She was looking at Mo when she said it.

"Well, don't let it get cold, folks," Della went on to the rest of the table. But no one moved.

"Calvin, have you tried—"

"It was your idea," Mo said in a low voice. "Your idea all along."

"Mimosa, honey," Della said with a plastered smile. "I told you I misspoke—"

"That's why you never came for me. That's why you never agreed when I said I'd run out by the road, you could pick me up, you'd never even have to come up to the house, never even have to *see* your sister."

Mo shook her head, trying in vain to deny the truth that had been there all along. It finally made sense.

"Mimosa, you're being silly—"

"Silly?" she said, her eyebrows shooting into the stratosphere. Her voice had sharpened with her perception.

Della looked around the table again.

"I... Rosie, won't you tell her—"

"No, Adelle, *love*. I won't tell her. You're her mother. You tell her."

Mo wondered briefly if Roz was enjoying this. But one

look at her face gave her the answer. There was disgust there and a fair amount of anger, but Mo could see no satisfaction in her aunt's eyes.

"Honey, you have to understand. It really was for the best."

"For the best? For the best that you shipped me off without a word? That you lied to me, again and again. I begged you, Mama. I begged you to come and get me."

"Mimosa, honey, you were only fourteen. I didn't think you'd understand—"

"I didn't! I don't understand *now*, and I haven't been fourteen in a long time!"

"This is exactly why I didn't tell you, Mimosa," Della said, going on a weak offensive.

"I knew you'd be mad and—"

"Mad?!" Mo could feel her temper bubbling up like lava as her world started to shift. "Mama, I wasn't mad. I was devastated!"

"Oh honey, don't be angry with me. Please, MoMo. You know how I hate to be yelled at."

A deep and ingrained need to set Della's mind at ease surfaced in Mo at her mother's words. She fought it back.

"Why, Mama?" she asked softly. "Why would you send me away?"

Della looked around her again, desperate now for someone to help her.

Roz sighed, then looked Mo square in the eye.

"Can you really not think of any reason? She sent you here because you were fourteen years old and pregnant. Pregnant by a man who had absolutely no intention of marrying you or taking care of you and the child you were carrying. It's not that difficult to comprehend."

"You sent me away because of the baby?" There was a deep, real hurt in her voice as she begged her mother for the truth.

"I... you... oh honey, you were only fourteen! You were just a baby yourself! And I certainly couldn't—"

"Couldn't what? Couldn't raise a baby? You wouldn't have had to! I'd been taking care of *you* for as long as I could remember!"

"Oh, but honey, babies! Babies are so very much work. You can't possibly understand."

Della reached across the table to take Mo's hands in hers, trying to justify to her daughter why she'd sent her away, carrying her only grandchild, to have that child miserable and alone in this pit of lies.

Mo snatched her hand away.

"I needed you. Your granddaughter needed you. How could you? *I* was your baby once. You found the perseverance to take care of me, but you couldn't do the same for my child?"

Della pulled her hands back, looking down at her lap. She glanced up at her sister, but Mo didn't know why she bothered to keep doing that. Roz was clearly not going to cover for her any longer.

But it wasn't Roz who broke the silence that fell around the table. It was Calvin.

"Isn't anyone going to tell her?"

"Tell me what?" Mo asked slowly. There was more?

Calvin looked at his sisters in turn. When neither spoke up, he turned to his niece.

"Della had no intention of raising a grand baby, Mo. And you're wrong. She didn't have the perseverance to raise a baby. Not any baby. Including you. You lived here, at Red Poppy until you were nearly three years old."

She shook her head, confused.

"But I knew that. I can remember that. We were happy here, until Roz threw us out."

"No, Mimosa," Calvin said gently. "*You* were happy here. Della wasn't here at all, for the majority of that time. It wasn't Della who raised you as a baby, Mo. It was Roz."

"But...but that can't be right."

The memories, the sunny, happy memories that had always lain at the base of herself, like a hand-quilted blanket placed in the bottom of a hope chest to keep everything else safe. Those memories were *real*. They were the realest, safest things she knew. Those were the memories that somehow made the ragged edges of the broken things stacked on top of them a little less sharp.

Horrified, Mo looked at Roz.

"It was you."

Her aunt didn't respond. She didn't need to. Because once Mo knew, she knew.

"There was no hidden stash of letters. No letters ever came, did they?"

After a moment's hesitation, Roz said, "No."

"MoMo, love, I—" Della said, trying to pull Mo's attention back to her.

The nickname grated on her raw nerves and Mo held a hand up to her mother.

"Stop talking," she told Della, then turned to her aunt.

"You let me hate you. I hated you," she said to Roz. "I *still* hate you."

"Better to hate me than know the truth and hate her. Or hate yourself, thinking you were somehow to blame for her shortcomings."

There was no softness in her words. There was no softness in her at all.

"But *why*?" Mo said quietly.

"Why what?"

"Why did you take me? I didn't understand it then, and I don't understand it even now. I wasn't a child, not one of your projects like Tate and Sadie. I was fourteen and pregnant, for God's sake. You didn't even want me."

"What's want got to do with anything, Mimosa? And you're wrong. You *were* a child. At one time you were *my* child. Do you think that goes away? And Della had no business, no business—"

Roz broke off.

"Go ahead, then. Tell her the rest," Calvin said. He looked at both of his sisters. Yet again, neither seemed willing to speak.

"No? I think she's dealt with enough from the two of you. Tell her the rest!"

Della winced, but still, nothing.

"Fine," Calvin looked at Mo.

"Roz is wrong, Mo. Want has plenty to do with it. And Roz *did* want you. She knew you'd despise her for what she was doing, but don't ever think she didn't want you. And Della knew it. So when my baby sister put a dollar amount on her daughter, Rosalind never hesitated."

Georgia gasped. Tate's mouth fell open. Even Otis looked at Della with shock on his useless face.

"Calvin, you take that back!" Della yelled. "That's not what happened. Why do you think any of this is your business anyway?"

Mo couldn't take it anymore. At this very moment, there was absolutely nothing more that she could take.

Without saying a word, she rose.

In front of her they were yelling at each other, each pointing a finger at the other, competing for the title of who was the worst person. Except for Roz, who was sitting in silence, watching her niece absorb the truth she'd always thought she wanted to know.

Della rose, too.

"I can see I'm unwelcome here. And in my own childhood home, too. This is—"

"Sit down," Roz said, her voice like a judge's mallet on the table. "You sit down now, Adelle. You made your bed a lot of years ago. Now you get to sleep in it. You came here. You did this. Now you sit."

And sit she did.

"No one is leaving this table until this is done," Roz said, looking at each of them in turn.

But Mo didn't care.

She had to get out of there.

She turned and left.

Out the front door and onto the porch, Mo leaned

against a post and closed her eyes, trying to block out what was going on behind her.

This time, when the memories came she let them. Anything to escape the circus in the dining room and the riots in her mind.

She was coming back to reality, slowly, hitting painful plateaus along the way, where her mind warned her to stop, but she fought against it.

"Mimosa."

It was her aunt.

"Give me my baby," she croaked, her voice papery and thin in her throat.

"The baby is dead, Mimosa."

She knew that. She knew. Did they think she didn't know?

"I want to see her. Where is she? Give her to me!"

She was frantic again, coming back with the last drop of fight she had left.

"Give her to me!"

There were hands. Another shot stinging her arm.

And blackness. Again.

"Mo."

It was Tate. He looked lost.

"Mo, I don't know what to do."

She didn't know if he meant what to do to help her, or what to do about the stinking abyss of people at the dinner table.

"Oh, Tate. You don't have to do anything. I'm sorry you had to hear all that."

Mo looked at this boy's confused face and knew he was hurting again, this time for her, and they were all responsible for it. It only served to fuel the fire burning her up from within.

"Tate, why don't you go up to your room, bud. You don't have to deal with any more of this."

He shook his head.

"I want to stay with you. Can't I stay with you?"

Mo thought of the custody paperwork waiting upstairs. Waiting for her.

She nodded.

"If you want."

Tate reached over to take her hand, and they made their way back to the dining room.

They were still arguing. Della was crying—an old trick.

"What is wrong with you people?" she heard Georgia say, shaking her head in disgust.

When Mo walked back into the room, they grew silent, watching and waiting for a reaction

"How much?" she asked quietly.

"Mimosa, love, we shouldn't be talking about this. Talking about money this way, it's in bad taste—"

Mo's eyes widened. She surprised them all, including herself, when laughter began to bubble up inside of her, spilling out. It started slow, a giggle, then grew larger, more uncontrollable. She couldn't stop it, in spite of the shocked faces around her, and she let it pour up and out of her. It echoed in the room, reverberating and repeating back on itself.

"Mo," Calvin said, concerned.

But another round of hysterical laughter took hold, and she laughed until tears were running down her face. The insane absurdity of it all had hit her and wouldn't let go.

There was nothing they could do but wait, letting the laughter take its course. When it finally slowed it trickled down to sniffles. Like a child falling from the dizzying heights of a sugar rush, the crash came right on its heels.

A sob took hold and pulled her down. But Mo wouldn't do it. She couldn't. Everything she had left in her fought against letting them see her brought to her knees.

"I want to know how much," she said slowly, quietly, wiping her face.

"How much did you pay her for me?" she said, directly to Roz. "How much was her daughter worth to her?"

"Mimosa," Roz said. "Why are you doing this?"

"How much, you bitch!" Her palm slammed onto the table, making the china clink and startling them all.

"Tell me!"

"More than she got the first time around," came a lazy, amused voice from the doorway behind Mo.

Everyone whipped around.

Arlo Vaughn knew how to make an entrance.

"Shut your filthy mouth," Roz hissed, looking rattled for the first time in this whole sorry episode.

"You really should lock your doors, hon," Arlo said, giving them all a slow smile. "Why, anybody could walk in right off the street."

"What do you mean, the first time?" Mo asked him, but she may as well not even have been in the room, for all the attention paid her. Roz and her former husband had eyes for no one but each other, like two cats circling one another with their backs arched. You could almost hear the deep warning rumble coming from Roz as the man unfolded himself from his slouch in the doorway and walked over, taking a good long look at the spread on the table.

"None of this is your business, Arlo. You need to let it lie."

"Now see, Rosie, girl, we can finally agree on something. It ain't none of my business. You're right."

He paused.

"You like that? Being right? I know you do. Unless you changed an awful lot, and aside from your unfortunate… predicament, I got a feeling you hadn't. I'd say that might be your favorite thing in the world, being right. Am I right?"

Roz didn't bother to respond but glared at Arlo as he leaned over and picked up an asparagus spear off of Mo's plate. He looked at it quizzically, wrapped in its cured piece of pork. He didn't take a bite but waved it around in his hand as he spoke.

"But see, here's the thing, Rosie, girl. You got something I want. So my business or not, I do believe I may need to use the knowledge I possess to... lee-verage the situation. You like that? That's a big, college word there, boy, you take note," Arlo said, directing the last bit at Tate, who was glaring at him.

"What is wrong with you, that you're made this way? You think it's funny to be so cruel?"

"Not cruel, Rosie," Arlo said, tossing the vegetable back on Mo's plate and wiping his fingers down his shirt. "Practical. Give me what I want, and you won't never see my face again. None of you will, even the fat man here that I ain't never seen before."

He nodded in Otis' direction.

"That chicken good, boy?" Arlo asked Otis. "You cleaned them bones like they was the cure for something, didn't you."

"I..." Otis looked around, surprised to find himself in the spotlight. But no one cared what he had to say.

"So, the way I see it, it's real simple. You give me what I want, Roz. We played these silly games long enough. Hand it over, and I'm outta here. And all your secrets go with me."

Arlo smiled, pleased with himself. He truly believed he'd found Roz's weak spot and he was enjoying poking at it with a stick.

But Mo knew better. Her aunt had no weak spots.

Roz had locked her jaw and was staring at the wall.

After a moment, she turned her head, dismissing Arlo and looking Mo straight in the face.

She wouldn't be played.

"Yes, Mimosa. I paid my sister for you. I knew she'd sell you to me. For enough money. I knew, because she'd done it before."

Della stuttered, "That's a lie! That's not—"

Arlo clapped Della on the shoulder, bending down to look her in the eye.

"Aw, come on now Della, honey. Did you forget? Red Beechum was a friend of mine."

Arlo had lost his leverage. He had nothing if Roz wasn't willing to reward him for keeping his mouth shut. But that didn't seem to bother him much. He had the soul of an anarchist, and he was reveling in every minute of this.

Arlo straightened back up.

"Yeah, I guess that slipped your mind. Red, man. That old boy was a pretty one, wasn't he? Why, I heard you tried it on with him yourself, a time or two. But you were a little old for his tastes, weren't you, Dell."

Arlo took a gander at Otis' plate, leaning down to pluck a grape for himself.

"Yeah, old Red. He liked 'em young."

He tossed the grape into his mouth and squeezed it between his back teeth.

Mo could do nothing but look on in horror.

Arlo liked being the master of ceremonies. He liked it a lot.

"You shut your mouth, Arlo Vaughn. You don't know nothing 'bout nothing," Della said. Her southern belle façade was breaking around her. The trailer park was showing through the cracks.

"Aw, Della, honey, that hurts me. I got feelings, you know. What about you, Mimosa? You want me to shut up?"

Mo stared at him, stuck on this ride that never ended. How she wanted it to end. But she wouldn't beg him. The stone in her face mirrored her aunt's, but Arlo was unfazed. He was relishing this.

"Yeah, see, Red he'd already gotten himself in a bind once before over a pretty young thing. Somebody's daddy didn't like what he was getting up to with his little girl. Broke his nose, if I remember right. And rightly so. That girl couldn't have been no older than twelve or thirteen."

Arlo shook his head as he circled the table, looking over their plates.

"Never understood it myself. His proclivities for the nubile ones. Awkward, really. Me, I prefer a woman with some experience. A woman who knows what she's doing, you know what I mean?"

He raised an eyebrow in Della's direction.

"I bet you know what I mean, fat man. Don't you. You know just what I mean."

Della looked ready to launch herself over the table and rip out Arlo's throat.

"Anyhow, Red wasn't one to take chances with his face, if he could avoid it. So when his eye alighted upon you, my dear, fresh as a daisy and just as sweet… Well, he knew Della here from way back. And he knew she might just be amenable to a little agreement. An exchange of goods and services, so to speak. For a little cold hard cash, of course."

And with those words, the fuse that had been lit reached the bomb he'd placed in the middle of the room. Everyone reacted at once.

Georgia looked at Mo with so much sorry in her face. She had two fingers held up to her lips, trying to hold it in. Mo didn't know how her friend didn't crumble under the weight of it. And while Mo sat there, dazed, trying to figure that out, Tate launched himself over her at Arlo. She managed to grab hold of him and hold him back. They were both shaking.

Della was up too, coming around the table at Arlo. Calvin stood abruptly, pushing his chair back and taking her by the arms to stop her, but he couldn't stop her mouth.

"That's not fair, that's not how it happened!" she screeched. "It was always her choice! It's not like he forced himself on her, she had a choice! She could've said no, but she didn't! I don't see why I ought to take the blame because she couldn't keep her legs closed!"

There was a sound like a shot ringing through the room when Calvin slapped her face.

Della gasped and put a hand to her cheek, pulling back from her brother.

Otis made a move, halfway picking his large frame up out of his chair.

"Hey now, you can't go hitting my girlfriend," he sputtered.

"Oh, shut up, Otis," Della yelled, turning her anger onto

him.

He looked unsure what to do now that he'd actually spoken and stayed there, half standing, half squatting, over his chair like a man who's had some bad eggs.

"Sit down," Georgia said, grabbing him by the arm and plunking him back into his seat.

Mo held tight to Tate, held him like the fellow shipwreck survivor he was, while the sharks circled around them.

Roz, for her part, sat as silent and staunch as on old Ironsides.

"Looks like ya'll decided to have a family reunion," came a new voice from the doorway. "Guess my invitation must've gotten lost in the mail."

Well now, looky here, Rosie. Our good for nothing son's decided to show his face. I'd call this a damn fine party."

Arlo grinned at her from the seat he'd taken in Della's chair and munched on a carrot.

Phillip looked gaunt and dirty. He had a desperate look in his eyes and lines on his face that Mo didn't remember being there.

"I need help. I owe people. And you owe me," Phillip said, ignoring Arlo and speaking to his mother.

"Back where we started, are we? The last time we had this conversation, Phillip, I ended up in the hospital after you left me for dead."

There was a collective gasp around the table. Even Arlo, turned his head, starting at Roz in shock.

"I thought you couldn't remember," Phillip said in a low voice.

But Roz had reached apparently terminal limit of prevarication she was willing to put up with for the day.

"Of course I remember, Phillip."

"But... but why—"

"Why what? Why did I keep my mouth shut instead of sending you to prison?"

"Mama, I don't know what to do. I'm desperate. I never meant—"

His voice caught, and he couldn't go on.

"I don't think you get it, Phillip," Roz said. "You may not believe this but I've spent a great deal of time in the last few weeks trying to decide what I can do to help you. And I don't know that there is anything."

"Mama—"

"Maybe you're this way by nature. Too much of your father in you. Maybe because I was a poor excuse for a mother to you. Probably both. But short of having you tossed into jail, where you'd no doubt learn to be a better criminal, I can think of nothing else. And for what it's worth, I can't seem to bring myself to do that."

Phillip let out a pent up breath.

"Thank—"

"Don't thank me. You never thanked me before. All those times you'd come here, looking for me to bail you out of whatever jam you'd put yourself in. Every time, I'd think of all the things you might have been, if only you hadn't been you and you hadn't come from me. And I *did* feel like I owed it to you. Because money was the only thing I ever had to give. It's not that I didn't try to love you, Phillip. I just didn't have it in me."

Such bald words were difficult to hear. But for once, Mo knew without a doubt that Roz wasn't lying.

"The only thing left to do is cut you loose. I should have done it years ago."

"You can't do that! I need your help! I owe people. You've got to help me!"

Phil's desperation was palpable. Still Roz was unmoved. Arlo rose and took his son by the arms and went to lead him out of the room.

"I can't do that," Roz said. "I'm sorry."

"Sorry?! You're not sorry! This is bullshit!" he yelled,

leaning around Arlo to get a look at Roz.

Arlo took one hand from Phillip's forearm and backhanded him.

"Grow up boy. Stop whining for your mama to get you out of trouble. It's time to take the tit out of your mouth."

Phillip was embarrassed and humiliated. Mixed with desperate, it was an ugly combination.

He pushed his father's hands off of his arms with an angry swipe. Mo thought Phillip might be about to take a swing at Arlo, but to her shock his face crumpled and big heaving sobs start choking out of him. He pulled his arm up to his face, hiding it in the crook, while his body shook and snot ran out of his nose.

"I think you should leave now," Roz said.

Phillip lifted his face, where the tears were making tracks in the grime.

"I should have killed you when I had the chance," he said, his face twisted and angry as he aimed the words at her like bullets from a gun.

"Then all the money you got squirreled away'd be mine. This is your fault," he said, pointing a finger at Roz.

"This is all your fault."

His finger jabbed at the air.

"This isn't over. Not by a long shot, Mama. Not until I say it is."

Phillip backed out of the room, and they all let out a breath.

"What a treat he is. No wonder you want a second chance at being a mother, babe. You did such a fine job with that one."

"Phillip did this to you?" Mo asked, shocked more deeply than she cared to admit.

"Of course he did, Mimosa. My God, girl, when are you going to start seeing people for what they really are?"

"But you've been protecting him. Why didn't you tell the police the truth?"

"Truth?!"

For once, Roz was visibly angry.

"What truth? The truth where I gave birth to a child who was so much like his father, all the way down to the bone, that I couldn't stomach the sight of him? The truth where I could see his future mapped out in front of him like a roadmap to prison?

"Or the truth where my worthless sister showed up and took the only decent thing in my life, the only thing I'd ever cared about and plucked it away like a dandelion, wasting it on trailer parks and Red Beechum, leaving me with nothing left inside to give, even when I had a boy who needed it more than anyone I'd ever met? The truth where I got no more than the son I deserved? Is that the truth you want, the one you worship so devoutly?"

Mo sat back in her chair, her eyes wide at her aunt's angry admissions.

"What *did* you do with all that money, Rosie?" Arlo said, like she hadn't spoken at all. "Surely you didn't use it all to bail out Phil."

"There's no money, Arlo! I told you years ago, you took it! You were drunk and high, and you beat me black and blue, then you took it all and I never saw it again."

Arlo looked her in the eye while she spoke, taking time to consider her words.

"You're a liar, Rosie. You always have been."

Roz sighed.

"You're one to talk, Arlo."

"But I stick to the small stuff, babe. You though, you're something else."

He shook his head, almost admiringly.

The two of them were looking at one another, another battle in a long-fought war of wills, which is why neither saw their son come back into the room.

But Mo did.

She saw Phil, wearing a look she'd never seen on his face.

And in his hand, something she had seen before.

It was the handgun he'd pointed at his friend.

"I wasn't gonna use it," he'd said then.

But this time, things were different.

"Flip!" Mo yelled, but she couldn't get to him. There was no time.

Without a word, he lifted the gun in his parent's direction and pulled the trigger.

When she came to again, it was dark outside and she was alone. Her mind was still blurry and all Mo knew was that she had to get out of this place.

As quietly as she could, she slid out of the bed and stumbled around, looking for her clothes. She couldn't find the ones she was wearing when the labor pains started. They'd no doubt been taken away, swept off with all the other signs of the hell she'd been through.

Like it never happened.

Moving gingerly to her dresser, Mo found some maternity pants to pull on over her post pregnancy belly that was deflated and flabby. She could feel pangs in places she knew little about, and she held tight to those feelings. They reassured her that she'd not imagined it all in some nightmarish fever. That she wasn't crazy.

Mo slipped out of the front door and down the porch steps, not knowing, not caring how long it took, or what sort of toll it might take on her body. She knew only one true thing. She was leaving this place.

She was going home.

Arlo's body fell slowly backward out of his chair when the bullet struck him in the face. When the body and the chair hit the floor, Della screamed, but it fizzled and died in the silence, when no one joined her.

Mo reached for Tate, realizing with a blossoming panic that he wasn't there next to her anymore. She swung her head wildly, needing to put eyes on him, to make sure he was safe.

But he was gone.

"Nobody moves," Phillip said, his voice high-pitched and strange.

The gun was shaking in his hand as he pointed it around the table. Della let out a little whimper when it passed her. She grabbed at Otis and hugged him tight, burying her head in his chest. Whether for comfort or in the hopes that his flabby mass would act as a human shield, Mo couldn't know.

When Phillip was sure everyone had heard him, he turned the gun on Roz.

"It didn't have to be this way, Mama. All I needed was a little help."

Her face was pale, her eyes shuttered low, but she looked calm.

"I know that, son. But I'm afraid my answer is the same. The help you need is not in my power to give."

Phillip's face quivered as he struggled to come to terms with her words. After all these years, he'd finally made his stand, demanding in this final way that his mother sit up and listen.

And still, sitting there with a loaded gun pointed at her head, with blood spatters on her face and clothes from the dead man on the floor next to her, even still, she held all the power.

Phillip didn't know what to do.

He glanced around the room, but Calvin was on the opposite side of the table, his hands flat upon the top. His knuckles were turning white, and he looked like he'd seize any opportunity to take Phil down.

When Phil's eyes found Mo, she spoke softly to him.

"Flip, please. Please put down the gun. You don't want to do this."

"Mo, man. I don't have any options left. Gant's gonna kill me. I didn't mean to hurt her, the whole thing just got out of hand."

He lowered the gun to his side. It hung there heavy in his

limp hand.

"I lost it, and when I realized what I'd done, I got scared and ran. I didn't mean for any of this—"

Mo could see Calvin tense from the corner of her eye. She knew he was about to make a move, but there was no way he could get to Phil in time.

He'll kill him, Mo thought.

And then she saw something that pushed her heart into her throat.

It was Tate.

He was standing in the doorway behind Phillip, and he was shaking like a leaf on a tree.

The shotgun wavered unsteadily in his hands.

"You need to leave now," Tate said, his voice as shaky as his hands.

Phillip turned with a look of surprise, but Tate didn't back down.

"Go on, get out of here."

Mo couldn't hear anything beyond the pounding of the blood in her ears. Her eyes stayed trained on the gun. Not the shotgun but the gun still hanging by her cousin's side. The one he'd used to kill his own father.

There was no time. She couldn't let Phil raise that gun. It couldn't happen.

At the precise moment Mo chose to make her move, Calvin sprang up as well. But they were too far away. The table was between them. Neither could get to Phil or Tate in time, but maybe they could distract Phil, turn his attention to back to them. Turn the gun back to them. Anywhere, Mo thought desperately, anywhere but Tate.

She realized in that split-second that she'd gladly sacrifice every last person in that room, if she could keep Tate safe.

Like a pack of lions, she and Calvin ran at Phil.

He saw them coming at him. Desperate and afraid, Phil made his choice.

He dropped the gun in his hand and lunged at the kid. Tate only had time to back up half a step before Phil was grabbing the barrel of the shotgun with both hands. Phil yanked the gun, pointing it up and pulling it toward himself. Tate hadn't lightened the death grip he had on the gun, and he fell forward.

The gun went off and plaster rained down on their heads. Mo and Calvin froze. They'd made it around the corner of the table, but they were still too far away to do any good. And now there was something else between them.

Phillip had Tate in a headlock with one arm and the shotgun in the other hand. He pulled the boy around so that Tate was situated between him and the rest of the room. Now he had a weapon, a hostage, and a doorway to his back.

"Phillip. Son, let the boy go," Calvin said in calm, precise words.

"I'm not your son!"

Cal held up both hands, trying to diffuse the situation before it got any further out of hand.

"No, no of course not," he said.

Phillip, who had only one hand to spare for the shotgun, tossed it up in the air and caught it with his free hand again, then pointed it toward Cal, his finger now positioned on the trigger. But Mo's concern wasn't the gun.

Tate's face was turning red. He couldn't breathe. Phil's grip around his neck was cutting off his air supply.

"Flip, look at him," she said gently. "He can't breathe. Is this really what you want to do, man? That boy's never done you any harm."

Mo's voice was steady, but inside, she was dying with each breath Tate couldn't take. The look of terror on his face was cutting her open.

Phillip glanced down and saw that Mo's words were true. His grip loosened, and Tate managed to suck in a great gasping breath.

In the next moment, it was difficult to know exactly what happened. Phillip must have taken her words to heart, realizing that no, his problem wasn't with this kid. It never had been. It was with his mother.

He lifted the shotgun and swung it around just as Mo leapt toward the pair, intent on breaking Phillip's hold on Tate.

The gun went off with a blast meant for Roz. But it wasn't Roz who landed bleeding on the floor.

When Phillip saw the blood, saw what he'd done to the only person in his family, maybe in his whole godforsaken life, who had ever given a damn about him, he dropped the gun.

"Oh God," he moaned.

"God, Mo, I'm sorry!" he said.

Everyone started moving at once. Della dragged a dumbfounded Otis out of his chair, trying to pull him out of the room. Georgia's chair scraped as she threw it back and ran toward Mo.

Phillip, horrified at what he'd done, panicked again. His grip had never loosened enough on Tate to let the boy escape, and he tightened it again, pulling Tate with him as he ran out the door.

Calvin moved toward the door to follow them, then undecided, turned back to Mo.

"Jesus, Mo, are you all right? Where are you hit?"

Georgia was helping Mo to her feet. Mo had taken part of the blast in her left arm, but she didn't have time to deal with that now.

"I've got to get Tate," she said, holding her right hand over the wound.

Calvin and Georgia's relief was palpable when they realized she wasn't going to die. At least, not yet.

But they didn't have time to discuss it, as Mo pushed past them, heading in the direction Phillip took.

"Mo, you can't go after him by yourself!" Georgia called to her retreating back.

"Stay here and call Wade," Calvin told Georgia, with a quick caress on the cheek. "She won't be alone."

And he raced out the door after his niece, leaving Georgia in a room full of family that didn't belong to her. One of them was dead, one was paralyzed, one was worthless, and the other was the most offensively selfish excuse for a human being she'd ever had the displeasure to be around. And her day job was stripping, so that was saying plenty.

As for the nurse, she'd disappeared into the shadows, nowhere to be seen.

When they made it to the front, both of them flying off the porch, they saw Roz's green international barreling up the driveway at a speed the old thing probably hadn't seen in decades.

Grateful she'd gotten into the habit of leaving her keys hanging in the ignition, as so many of them did out here in the middle of nowhere, Mo ran for her jeep.

"You better let me drive," Cal called. With her arm in an undetermined state of chewed-up and bloody, she couldn't argue, so Mo climbed into the passenger side.

"Hurry, I don't want to lose him," she told Cal, but the direction was unneeded. The jeep fishtailed as Cal swung it around after Phil and Tate, following the taillights that shone brightly in the dim evening light. Night had been busy falling while they'd played games with life and death.

The thought crossed Mo's mind that Calvin might be one of the only people in the world she could depend on. For an old stoner who'd never held a real job and came from the same family of winners that she did, it was a little bit of a miracle.

"There he is, he's turning," she said.

"I see him," Cal said softly, concentrating on the road and the jeep beneath him.

Georgia could do a lot worse, she thought. If, that is, they made it out of this mess without getting dead. If Phil kills Cal, I might as well let him take me out too, Mo thought. Because Georgia's never gonna get over that.

Suddenly, the tail end of the old truck—which had the

perseverance of a mule and about as much speed, thank God—veered off the road to the right.

"Where's he—"

"Oh, Jesus," Mo said. "Hurry Cal. You've got to hurry."

Mo knew that turn off. It looked like nothing but woods from the road, overgrown as it was with brush. But all it took was one look at the trees—or lack thereof—to know what was what. They'd been cleared over a hundred years before, to make way for the trains that used to run down the tracks that were still there, hiding under a shallow blanket of dirt and pine needles.

Trains that had long since stopped running on those abandoned tracks. Then, of course, there was that one time those tracks been used to lead a stolen police cruiser through the woods on either side, straight to the rickety trestle bridge that still stood precariously over the river below.

"He's headed for the bridge, Cal."

"But there's a gate, he can't—"

They heard the smashing, grinding crunch of metal on metal up ahead.

"He did."

"But why? He's got nowhere to go."

Mo saw the truck ahead, tangled in the metal gate. The faithful old bull had almost made it through. She sent up a silent prayer of thanks to anyone who might be up above listening that the gate had done its job.

The bridge rose out of the evening ahead of them, all weathered wood and rusted metal.

"Because that's where you go when you've got nothing left to lose," she said, as she threw open the door of the jeep and ran toward the truck, with Calvin on her heels.

And still, they were two very important steps behind Phillip.

He'd already managed to wrest open the door of the truck and was pulling Tate out with him, holding him close to his body like a shield.

"Phillip! Stop, Phil!" she called, but he moved faster at the sound of her voice. The night had gotten darker in just the last few minutes, and Mo saw to her horror that a fog was starting to roll in.

I take it back, she thought about her prayer, as she watched Phillip drag Tate back into the mist that had begun to envelop the bridge.

"Don't, Mo," Phil called. "Don't come out here."

"Let the boy go, Phil, and you can dance out there naked for all I care."

She heard a short bark of laughter.

"That's right. None of you ever gave a damn about me, did you?"

"That's not true Phil, and you know it."

She could barely make out the darkened shapes ahead, but that meant Phil couldn't see her clearly either. She moved forward, trying to make up some of the distance.

"Yeah? You know what I know, Mo? I know my parents never loved me. My dad never even bothered to hate me. He didn't care enough for that."

"Stop feeling sorry for yourself, Flip. So you had crap parents. So what. So did I. Apparently my mother used me as a commodity for cash, and I don't have the first clue who my dad even was."

"Mimosa!" Cal hissed behind her. "Don't antagonize him, you idiot."

"If I give him anything else, he's gonna know I'm lying," she whispered back. God, how she hoped she was doing the right thing. More than one life might depend on it.

"You talk to him, then. And stay here. Keep him distracted, focused on you," she told Cal.

"What are you gonna—"

"You don't get it, Mo. You never did," Phil called through the fog, moving farther and farther out onto the bridge.

Mo nodded her head sharply at her uncle and waved her hand in a circular motion. Keep him talking.

"She *doesn't* get it, Phil, does she?" Cal called back. "She couldn't."

Mo nodded, then faded off to the left side of the bridge. Calvin didn't have time to ask her what she thought she was doing.

"Cal?"

"Yeah, it's me, man. Look, it's not Mo's fault. It's just real hard to see past your own crap. And the girl has had plenty thrown at her."

"And I haven't?"

"I'm not saying that. Not by a long shot."

Cal had a brighter future than she did when it came to hostage negotiation, Mo thought as she crouched down, keeping her good hand on the planks that lined the train tracks. When she found her way to the place where the ground gave way to the rocky outcroppings below, she reevaluated her previous statement to the powers that be.

I take it back again, she thought. I'm fine with the fog. Really. Good call. In fact, make it thicker, if you want. But please, God, please, let this work.

"You don't know what it's like, Cal. Neither of you do."

"You're right. You're absolutely right," Cal called.

Mo could barely make out his form, but his voice carried on the still night air.

"It's so hard, man. When nobody believes you're worth a damn, why the hell should you be?"

Oh, spare me, Mo thought, rolling her eyes as she moved gingerly down the rocky slope. Hooking her good right arm over the bridge planks and gripping the edge of the wood with her hand, she prayed harder this time. She lifted her knees, testing her strength, and closed her eyes tight. Her body swung toward the tracks a bit, but she held on for dear life.

"Phil, buddy, believe me, I don't know how you came out of that house sane. Nobody's gonna blame you for snapping the way you did. Hell, we could go back there now, load up Arlo's body in the truck and bury it by the river.

Nobody's gonna miss the guy."

Not knowing if it was a good thing that Cal was giving Phil an out—as unrealistic as it might be—or a bad thing that he was reminding him he'd just murdered his own father, Mo could only hope Cal could keep up the chit-chat for however long this was going to take.

"That's never gonna work," Phil called.

"It will, Phil. It will, man. But you've gotta do something first."

"I can't let the kid go, Cal. He's the only thing I got left."

And those words helped Mo find the strength to swing up with her bad arm, the one that was steadily leaking blood down the left side of her body. She curled her fingers around a plank two up from the one she was hanging onto and got right with the Lord.

"It'd be a gesture of good faith, Phil. Proof you're thinking with your head. The kid doesn't need to be in the middle of this."

"I can't Cal. Man, I can't. When you go through life and you're nothing, you learn, real fast, that the only way you're gonna keep people's attention is to have something they want. Something they need."

"I just want to hear his voice, Phil. Let me hear his voice."

Before Mo could think too hard about the rocks below or the growing gap between them and her feet, she took a deep breath and put her weight on her injured left arm, sliding quickly down the tracks with her right.

It took everything she had not to cry out. The pain was un-freaking-imaginable. She wavered, her legs swinging wildly beneath her.

But it worked. She was two feet closer to Tate than she'd been before.

So she focused all her will on that and did it again.

"He's fine, Cal. I'm not gonna hurt a kid. What kind of person do you think I am?"

"I know you don't want to hurt the boy, Phil. I know that, deep down, like I've never known anything else. Just let me hear his voice. It'll make me feel better and the kid, too."

"So talk, kid," she heard Phil say.

"Cal? Tell Mo—"

"She's right here, Tate. She can hear you," Cal said quickly. Too quickly.

"Tell her I'm sorry, I didn't mean—"

"Mo, you're awful quiet, babe," Phil called out.

She was coming closer, two feet at a time. Her left arm was screaming, and she couldn't see past her face, but she could hear Phil and Tate's voices. They were louder than they'd been before. Just a little closer.

"She's upset, Phil. We both are. We're worried about Tate, and we're worried about you, man. You need to come off of there. It's not safe."

"Where's Mo, Cal?" Phil called.

She was close enough to hear his footstep as he backed further out onto the bridge. She struggled to move faster, making up the distance, while her arm came close to its breaking point.

"Right here, man. She's right here. Talk to me, brother," Cal said. "Keep talking to me. We can fix this. We can make this right."

"Where the hell is Mo, Cal? I better hear her voice real fast, or I can't be held responsible for what's gonna happen."

"She went back, Phil," Cal said. "She went back to get help. She wants to help you."

Mo's left arm had lost all feeling. She didn't know how much longer she could expect it to hold her. She willed her fingers to curl around the board, knowing this was her breaking point. What she didn't know, what she couldn't know, was whether it was enough to stop Phil, as she hoped, or stop her life on the rocky edge of the river below.

"Went back to call her boyfriend the cop, you mean."

With all the strength she had left to muster, Mo started swinging her body back and forth, letting all her hopes rest on her good arm, demanding it do the job of two. When she thought she was as ready as she'd ever be, she brought up her leg, trying to hook it over the planks.

And she came up short, her body swinging back like a pendulum.

It wasn't going to work, she realized. It was all for nothing. She was going to die here, which was probably no more than she deserved. She'd had one job. One. To take care of those kids. And she'd let each and every one of them down.

"Wade's not so bad, Phil. Wade's always been a friend," she heard Cal say in the distance.

But it was the whimper of fear that reached her from the bridge that gave her the push she needed to try one last time. With silent tears leaking out of her eyes, Mo pushed away the pain and found bedrock. She hoped this worked, because she had nothing left.

With one final push, her leg swung up and caught.

"A friend to who? Not to me, man. To Mo maybe, but everyone's a friend to Mo. They all want to get close to her, thinking some of that... whatever it is she's got will rub off on them. Growing up next to Mo was almost as bad as growing up with Roz. Nobody even bothered to look at me! Not you, not my friends, not even my own damn mother!"

Mo's anger at Phil's words gave her the final bit of strength she needed to pull her body up from its brutal suspension over the rocks that waited hungrily below. She rolled onto the bridge, trying her damndest not to make too much noise. Moving into a crouch, she saw the powers that be had a sense of humor after all. She'd managed to come up right before one of the large beams that rose to hold the trestle overhead.

Phil hadn't seen her. Not yet.

Mo pulled herself into a ball, scooting closer to the beam on her butt, leaning her back against it.

"She won't make it, Cal," Phil said.

He was close. She'd made up some of the distance he'd

managed to put between them, but she couldn't know how much. She couldn't know if it would be enough.

"She'll never make it back here in time. Tell her...tell her..." Phil trailed off.

Mo knew it was now or never. She stood and stepped out away from the beam. The planks creaked under her weight, but they held. At least, for the moment.

"Tell me what, Phil? I'm right here, you can tell me yourself."

Startled, Phil pulled Tate tighter to him, backing away from Mo like she was a ghost that had materialized from nowhere.

"Where the hell did you come from?" Phil yelled, his eyes wide and wild.

Mo raised her hands, trying to calm him down. He was pulling Tate too close to the edge of the tracks, and his grip wasn't loosening. She took two cautious steps toward the pair. They were still so, so far away. She needed him to calm down. Now.

"Flip, don't do anything crazy. It's all gonna be fine."

"It's not! Don't talk to me like I'm a child, Mo! It's not fine, it won't be fine, it has *never* been fine!"

Phil wasn't calming down.

She saw him glance behind him, down at the river below. With the fog obscuring her sight, Mo had no idea if they were far enough out to be over water or rocks. But she could see Tate's face, could almost taste the fear coming off him in waves. He had both hands up, gripping Phil's arm where it held him in a death grip. But the kid was smart, he didn't struggle, didn't kick or bite. He didn't do anything that would give Phil any reason to stumble or fall.

It was up to Mo.

But her plan hadn't extended as far as figuring out how to get Tate safely away from Phil. And now, with the two of them balancing on the edge of nothing, she could see few choices.

"Please, Flip, I'm begging you, please let the boy go."

Phillip looked at her. She'd come closer. Phil and Tate were out of her reach, just a few more steps. She needed just a few more.

She may not have been close enough to grab Tate, but she was close enough to see Phil's face. She saw when the panic-fueled anxiety drained from his face like someone emptying a glass. She saw all too clearly the deep and unrelenting sadness that remained.

"I'm sorry, Mo."

"NO!" she cried.

But there was nothing she could do. Phil released his hold on Tate, and his hands floated out to his sides, forming an unholy tribute to the son of the Lord. They say time slows down at the crossroads of life and death, but up until this moment, Mo had never found that to be the case. But as she watched Phil lean backwards, falling into the fog and whatever was waiting on the other side of it, her limbs felt like they'd never been so heavy, so slow to respond to the synapses her brain was blasting at them.

To her dying breath Mo would believe that Phillip only ever intended to take himself over that edge, leaving Tate to run back into her arms to safety and security. But in typical Phil fashion, he screwed it up.

Tate's sudden freedom threw him off balance. Mo watched, horrified, as he pitched forward, then overcorrected, his arms whirling.

At the same time that Phil's boots disappeared silently into the mist, Tate struggled to stay on his feet.

But it was a losing battle. Tate was falling, following Phil over the side.

Without thought, without any weighing of the pros and cons or examining her options, Mo did the only thing it was in her to do.

She launched herself after him.

Mo hitchhiked the last part of the way, though if the middle-aged trucker had any ideas about her being good company, of any sort, he was wrong. Mo watched the miles go by in silence, counting the minutes that took her further from Red Poppy, further from her aunt. But she couldn't escape the sounds in her head. Especially the sound of a baby that never cried.

The trucker dropped her at the highway exit she indicated. It wasn't far now.

The walk that followed, through the night, was hard on her body. She should be in bed, she knew. But she didn't care.

Mo almost managed to feel relief at the sight of the sign that hung above the entrance to the trailer park. But her mind felt like it'd been frozen in ice, and she was too numb to feel anything at all.

There was no joy that greeted her when she caught sight of the trailer on lot number four, the one she'd moved into with Della nearly three years ago—a lifetime in Della years.

And when she opened the door and found the place dark, empty and abandoned, there was no anger. No pain. No fear.

There was nothing.

When Roz found her an hour later, Mo was curled up in the corner of what was once her mother's bedroom on an old, stained mattress that was one of the only things left behind. The trailer that had once been her home had been cleared of everything else save a crumpled fast food wrapper in the corner of the room.

Mo wasn't sleeping. Just staring at a spot on the wall. But she barely registered Roz was there.

She'd given up.

"Get in the car, Mimosa. It's time to come home."

But Red Poppy wasn't her home. And neither was this. Not anymore.

She had no home anymore.

She could have made it harder on her aunt. Argued or refused. But what was the point?

In the car, she leaned her head against the glass of the passenger side window and watched the night go by again.

"The baby's been cremated. Her ashes scattered in the river."

Her aunt wasn't known for pulling her punches.

"You had no right," Mo whispered, finding her voice.

"It's better this way."

"Better for who?" she asked, lifting her head to stare at Roz, who was gripping the wheel tightly in both hands, her eyes pointing straight ahead.

"Now you can heal."

"Go fuck yourself," Mo said, dropping her head back against the glass.

The rest of the drive passed in silence.

When the car pulled into the driveway of the hated red house, Roz cut the engine. They both sat for a moment, staring out the front windshield, listening to the hot car engine tick as it cooled.

"I'll never forgive you," Mo said with no emotion whatsoever.

There was no answer for a moment, and Mo was reaching for the door handle when her aunt spoke.

"I can live with that," she said.

Mo knew the river below. Knew it intimately. And she knew they only had one chance, as slim and weak as it might be. In that split-second, without considering how very, very much could go wrong, Mo took a running leap at Tate, hitting him with all her force and forward momentum.

She held tightly, closing her eyes and thinking in that moment as they flew through the air, that no matter what happened, at least he'd know he wasn't alone.

When they hit with the force of a truck, it was only the cold that let her know they'd missed the rocks, landing miraculously in the river.

She could feel Tate pushing water around beside her and followed suit, holding her breath while they struggled to find the surface, guided only by intuition and a will to live.

And live they did.

As their heads broke the surface, nearly simultaneously, they were able to pull large heaving breaths into their lungs.

"Tate, oh God, Tate," she coughed and sputtered. "Are

you all right?"

Eyes wide with shock, he could only nod.

"Oh Jesus, come here," she said, pulling him close in a hug as they treaded water. Looking around for the nearest shore, Mo saw how dangerously nearby it was.

And there lay the broken body of her cousin. With an image of Nat in her mind, overlaying the one in front of her, she could find no anger. Only sadness. Sadness at a reckless, wasted life.

When Tate saw Phil's body, he clutched her harder.

"You saved my life," he said. "You came after me, and you saved my life."

Both sets of eyes were pulled back to where Phil lay.

"I'm sorry," Tate said. "I'm sorry, I'm sorry."

"Shh," she said, pulling them both up to the shore.

Tate was sobbing now, shaking with cold and wet and shock.

"I just wanted to be a hero," he said, his voice breaking while he babbled on. "I knew he was a bad guy. I knew. I saw him push Sadie's dad, and I didn't say anything. I was afraid. I should have said something."

"Shh, kid. Shh."

She held him tight, with their clothes plastered to them and river water streaming down their cheeks. She held him until the tears began to wane.

But the memories. Those would never go away.

"You still want to be a hero, kid?" she asked in a low voice.

He looked up at her face, which was growing paler by the minute.

"Now's your chance. Cal's up there somewhere. Go get some help, because I feel a little faint."

PART V

HOMECOMINGS AND GOINGS

Two days later

Mo walked Hayes to the door.

"With all the business that's gone around here, you do realize I pulled off a miracle, don't you?"

"Thank you, Hayes," she said.

His eyes widened in surprise. Doubtless, not a phrase he'd heard often in this house.

"Well," he said, "it helps to be friends with the judge. And the fact that you risked your life to save that boy didn't hurt."

He gave a meaningful look toward the sling holding up Mo's left arm.

"I'll be in touch," he said.

Mo shut the door behind him.

Sadie and Tate were curled up on the living room floor in sleeping bags while a movie played in the background. The remnants of the celebratory popcorn and cake were scattered about them, and Mo picked up paper plates and juice cups.

Without any ability to stop herself, she kneeled down and brushed Sadie's curls back from her face. Then she tucked the sleeping bag tighter around Tate.

For two kids who'd suffered through the prior weeks like heavyweight champs, they looked so very young in sleep.

But she knew they'd carry scars from this forever, wherever life took them. Knew it well.

Mo deposited the refuse in the kitchen. Georgia had moved into Cal's place, the two of them deciding that life was too short to waste time.

In a bald-faced move full of delusional moxie, Della and Otis were still around. Mo could only marvel at the woman's nerve. She was sure her mother had an agenda, if she'd chosen to stick around and endure the awkwardness her presence created. The situation would have to be dealt with soon enough. But for the moment, the pair were out partaking of what little nightlife Justus had to offer.

Mo found herself alone.

Well, almost.

She picked up the manila envelope Hayes had brought with him earlier when he'd delivered Sadie home to them, along with the matching pair that lay with it.

When she walked to the door of Roz's room, she saw that Iona was nowhere to be seen. Where the woman disappeared to all the time was a mystery. Not one Mo cared enough about to ask.

Roz had her eyes closed, but she opened them when Mo walked in and laid the two envelopes on the dresser.

"It's done," she said. "You got what you wanted."

"You signed them?"

"Yes."

Roz didn't speak. She didn't smile. But her face relaxed, the closest thing to approval Mo was going to get.

"Did you think I'd hold them over your head? Something you wanted, for something I want?"

"The thought crossed my mind," Roz admitted.

"It crossed mine, too."

Mo's brow furrowed and she ran a hand along the dresser picking up an old framed tintype. It showed a man with a cocky grin and a prim looking woman in fancy clothes. The ferryman and his wife, perhaps.

Setting it down, she turned back to her aunt who was watching her, waiting to hear what she had to say.

"I'm terrified," Mo said.

"As you should be."

"What if I can't be what they need me to be? What if I let them down?"

It felt strange to speak with Roz this way, seeking advice, confirmation she was doing the right thing.

"I'm sure you will."

Mo shook her head.

"That's a lot of help, really. I don't know what else I expected."

"You'll let them down. You'll fail. You'll make mistakes."

Mo threw up her hands and turned to leave the room.

"Then you'll get up the next day, and you'll try again. You'll do what you need to do, Mimosa."

Mo turned back to her aunt.

"You'll do what you have to do. Whatever you have to do. You'll do it, because you don't have it in you to do anything less."

Mo stared into her aunt's eyes. She saw the conviction there in her hard gaze. And she gave herself permission to hope Roz was right. She nodded.

"Will you tell me the truth about Lucy?"

God, how she hated to ask this woman for anything.

"Rosalind, I need to know."

"You are relentless, Mimosa."

"Don't you think you owe me that?"

Roz sighed.

"Yes. I do. But I'm tired. Ask me another day."

As it turned out, there was no other day. The next day, Rosalind Mabry was dead.

She'd left a note dictated by Iona, who'd disappeared into the woodwork for the last time. The note had instructions for what to do with her remains as well as instructions to gather everyone to view a videotape left sitting next to it.

After the ambulance had come and gone, taking the body away, they did just that. The room was quiet, save for Della's occasional choked sobs.

The faces in the room ran the gamut. There was shock, of course.

And looking around, Mo saw more grief than she might expect. Calvin looked devastated as he sat close to Georgia on the living room sofa. He'd never experienced a day in his life that his older sister hadn't been there, a rocky cliff to break the harsh wind.

Tate and Sadie were pale and silent, having lost the only security they'd ever known. All they had now was Mo. Having reconsidered her stance on a fickle God after the events at the bridge, she prayed she was up to the job.

Oddly, it was the lawyer who looked the most grief-stricken. There was a hitch in his voice, and he could barely bring himself to say Roz's name.

"Let's get to it, then," Hayes said hoarsely, inserting the tape into the ancient VCR.

The room was so silent that when the machine sucked in the tape they could hear the whirring of the gears on the video begin to unspool.

The screen on the television flickered grey and black static, then Roz came into view.

"—Red light blinking?" she said, squinting off to the left of the screen, in an inelegant beginning.

Her nurse and friend must have nodded, and Roz turned her attention to the center of the camera.

"Hayes, you may consider this video an extension of my

last will and testament. You'll find the paperwork in my dresser drawer. I believe it to be in order. You'll have to forgive the lack of my signature, as I no longer have use of my hands, but Iona has signed my name, with my knowledge and consent, and I have witnessed the words that were dictated upon the page by me and only me. I do expect that, with the addition of this video, that will suffice in the eyes of the law."

Mo was watching Hayes' face, as he drank in the sight of Roz on the screen, directing him in such businesslike tones. She wondered if Roz would have been surprised by the loss that pulled his features low.

"As to my death, let me assure each and every one of you that this is my choice and mine alone. I have no plans to live this way, trapped unmoving in my bed for an indefinite number of years. Absolutely no one else is to be held responsible. I have orchestrated and committed the act alone."

Managing to bring a bottle of pills to her mouth and swallow them in their entirety was a neat trick, for a quadriplegic, Mo thought. She assumed Iona and Roz had made arrangements for the nurse to disappear. Mo tried to picture her, somewhere on a beach in Florida with her brown polyester pants rolled up to the knee, sipping a drink with an umbrella. The absurdity of it brought an inappropriate laugh up to her throat. She pushed it down.

"Calvin," Roz said. "Thank you. I don't know that I ever said it in life, but I love you. I'm leaving you no formal bequest. You're a rare individual who's found what they need in what they already have. I respect that."

Cal's jaw was tight. Mo could see him swallow back emotions at words he'd never heard from his older sister in her lifetime.

"Adelle," Roz said in a harder tone.

Della sat up straighter, leaning toward the screen. Her sobs had given way, replaced by naked greed.

"You've taken enough from me. You'll get nothing

more. Perhaps God will have mercy on your soul, but you don't deserve forgiveness from me."

Della sucked in an outraged breath, looking around the room for support, but there was none to be had.

Roz moved on.

"Tate, the old international truck is yours. I understand it needs some work, but it'll pull through. And once it does, I'll have given you two things you can count on. That's more than many have."

Tate knew Roz was referring to Mo, and he held her hand tightly, clearly struggling to hold back tears.

"Sadie, my dear girl. I wish…"

Roz paused, overcome with an emotion that to Mo looked like regret, as her aunt struggled to find words. She'd never seen Roz overcome by anything, and she couldn't look away. But her aunt's determination won out, and she pulled herself together.

"The painting in your room, the one we hung there together of the poppies that you liked so much—it's yours to remember me by."

Sadie was crying silent tears, leaning her head against Tate. She buried her face in his shoulder, grieving in her sad, quiet way. She'd lost so much in so few years.

"Mimosa Jane," Roz went on, her voice back to its usual no-nonsense tone.

"The business and all its assets, the land, the house, and the entirety of its contents are your problem now. Treat them with a little respect, if you can manage it. There's a lot of history here."

Roz paused, and Mo waited, vibrating with tension. That couldn't be all. There had to be more.

As if reading her niece's mind, all too aware that Mo cared little to nothing for land or possessions or a house she'd always hated, Roz went on, addressing the one thing Mo needed from her. Needed it like she needed breath in her lungs or water in a parched desert landscape.

"Mimosa, I know you don't want to hear this, but there

are some things that are best left buried."

"No," Mo whispered.

"Let it lie, Mimosa Jane. It's for the best."

Roz nodded, and the video went to static.

"How dare you?" Mo said. "From the grave? How dare you?!"

All heads had turned in her direction. She didn't care. She'd never known anger like this in her life.

"Mimosa—" Hayes said

"Don't. Just don't"

She rose and left the room.

Three days later

The funeral was over.

It'd been a somber affair, punctuated by Della's dramatic bouts of tears. Many of the locals who had come to pay their respects to Roz, remembered Della. Some even gave her the spotlight she craved.

"What's going to happen to the house, Della? Are you planning to stay there?" one woman asked after the graveside service—a strikingly inappropriate question given the occasion, in Mo's opinion.

"Well, I don't see how Mimosa can do it all on her own, with those two little ones and all," Della replied.

Mo wondered if her mother even remembered their names.

Something's going to have to be done about her, Mo thought. But it was neither the time nor the place.

The two "little" ones were comporting themselves with more dignity than Della had ever shown in her sorry life, Mo thought. Standing side by side, in pressed clothes and shined shoes, she knew both of them felt the loss of Rosalind Mabry more deeply than anyone else present.

She herself had been sorely tempted to skip the whole

ordeal. She found her anger at her aunt hadn't lessened with the passing of the days but sharpened to a fine razor's edge.

In the end, she attended, because Sadie and Tate needed her. That was her role now.

She stood silently, nodding as people she didn't remember passed by, expressing their condolences at her loss. Each time they did, she was reminded of her true loss, and a baby that had no grave or headstone carved with her name.

With the kids quietly by her side, they walked away from the gathered mourners and found the spot where Emma had been buried next to her mother. The headstone hadn't been placed yet, the one Mo had chosen a matter of weeks ago. When the carvings were completed, they'd be back to this place. They'd bring flowers again, just as they did today.

Sadie placed the bouquet of daisies they'd chosen at the florist across the foot of her grave.

"Can we go home now, Mo?" Sadie asked quietly.

"There's a reception at the church after this. Do you want to go to that?"

Sadie shook her head.

"Do we have to?" Tate asked, glancing over his shoulder at the crowd of people who'd mostly ignored them, speaking only to the adults over their heads.

Mo placed her hand on his mousy head.

"No, we don't have to," she said. "We can go now, if you like."

The kids had been through enough for one day.

She drove them back to Red Poppy, leaving Della to play hostess at the church, a role she'd relish, Mo knew.

The two of them disappeared to their respective rooms to shed the uncomfortable funeral clothing, and Mo did the same.

Dressed again in their cutoff jean shorts and faded T-shirts, they found Mo on the porch, staring up the road.

"We're gonna go check on the kittens," Tate told her.

She nodded, and they were gone, leaving her to her solitary thoughts.

Mo rose and followed where her feet took her. Invariably, that was the river.

She sat on the bank and watched the water flow by.

This might be her favorite place on earth. Right here in this spot, where the water was so close you could kick off your shoes and walk down to it, with the clay and mud squishing through your toes. Not like the rocky shores that provided stability for the trestle bridge farther downriver and could do so much damage to a body who forgot to respect their purpose.

It was this spot that was carved upon her heart. She felt like she could have been born here. And she'd died a thousand deaths here.

When she died for the final time, she knew she wanted no headstone to mark the place where her body decayed. She wanted nothing more than the towering pines standing sentry at the water's edge when her ashes were scattered here.

As her daughter's had been.

Mo closed her eyes and leaned back to let the sun filter through the trees and warm her face.

Somehow, in that place, she was able to begin to come to terms with that.

Only the birds marked the time passing and the sun moving across her face. After a while, she heard a car door slam in the distance.

With a last regretful glance at the river, she rose and walked back to the red house where she'd never found the same sort of serenity.

"We'll need to rearrange some of the furniture in there, Otis. You can get started on that. Get the boy to help you," she heard her mother say, as the pair of them walked up the porch steps and into the house that Mo now owned.

She shook her head.

"What are you gonna do about her?" Cal asked.

He and Georgia had stepped out of his truck and stopped when they'd seen Mo coming up from the path to the river.

"I don't know yet," Mo said truthfully.

Georgia opened her mouth, clearly in possession of an opinion on the subject, then she shut it again.

Cal put an arm around Georgia's shoulders, giving her a small smile.

"Whatever you decide," he said to Mo, "I've got your back."

"Yeah, I guess you do. That means a lot, Cal."

"You're a good kid, Mo. You're gonna do fine."

Mo hoped his confidence was warranted. Herself, she had her doubts.

As the two of them walked toward Cal's place, Mo turned to head back into the big house, but she'd only taken a few steps when she was brought up short by the sound of someone trying not to be heard while they cried.

Someone whose skinny legs were hanging out of the bed of the beaten up green international truck.

Mo walked slowly toward the back of the truck. She didn't want to startle him. Peeking her head around the corner, she saw Tate swipe at his face, trying to wipe away the evidence of his tears.

"Hey," she said gently.

"Hey, Mo," he said. If she'd ever seen a face with so much sadness and so much worry in such a small space, she couldn't think of when.

Tate's shoulders were slumped and his already small frame was folded in on itself. Mo had seen him sad. She'd seen him angry, she'd seen him full of fear, and she'd seen him grieve. But she'd never seen him look like this. Like he'd given up.

"Can I sit down?"

He shrugged, so she slid onto the flatbed next to him.

Mo didn't push. She knew he'd talk if he wanted. When he was ready and not before, so she sat in silence next to him, her legs swinging off the truck next to his.

Eventually he spoke.

"Are you gonna leave now?"

She looked at him. He wouldn't meet her eyes. He knew about the custody paperwork; she'd told him after Sadie had come home. But it would take a lot more than a signature on a piece of paper to convince Tate of anything.

She reached over and put a hand on his shoulder. He lifted his eyes to hers.

"Anything I say to you right now, it's all just words. And words are hard to trust. Nothing will fix that except time. But I will say this. You're stuck with me now, Tate. You and Sadie both. Because whether you know it or not, I need you even more than you need me."

"What about your baby, though?" he asked.

The question jolted her.

"What about her?"

"What if you find her, then you'll have a kid of your own. A real kid. Then Sadie and me, we'll just be in the way."

Mo wondered if there would ever come a day when she didn't feel like her heart was on fire.

"My baby is dead," she said gently. The words hurt, but there was a hard won acceptance in them.

"She died a long time ago."

"But—"

"Shh," she told him when he broke off and started to cry. She pulled him to her and let him cry on her shoulder.

"Shh. It's okay. I'm not gonna lie, this scares me too. But we'll figure it out Tate. We'll figure it out as we go."

Avoiding Della had become a habit. One that it was time to break. Mo had no idea what her immediate plans were for she and the two kids. They could stay here, in the only home that had ever provided any sense of stability—and that was using the term loosely—or they could make a fresh start in a new place that didn't hold reminders around every corner of all they'd lost.

All Mo knew for sure was that she needed the time and

space for them to figure that out together, just the three of them, without the distraction of her mother and her baggage of a boyfriend hanging around.

Steeling herself for what was bound to be an unpleasant conversation, Mo went to find Della.

Heading down the hallway to the larger bedroom that Della and Otis had taken as their own, Mo heard voices coming from the room ahead.

"Why don't you come over here and sit on my lap?" she heard Otis say. Mo rolled her eyes. That was just what she didn't need, to interrupt those two getting friendly.

Mo considered turning back, but putting this long overdue confrontation off for the sake of her mother's afternoon tryst was a nauseating proposition.

Loudly, she knocked on the door, which hadn't been latched all the way. To her embarrassment, the door swung open, which wasn't at all what she'd wanted, intending only to give the couple some warning that they had a visitor.

There was a flurry of movement in the room, but not soon enough for Mo to misunderstand exactly what was going on here.

Otis stood quickly from the bed, and the person who fell off of his lap, nearly losing her footing in the process, wasn't Mo's mother.

It was Sadie.

"Hey, Mo," Sadie said.

"Hey, Sadie," she said, her voice calm and conversational. "I've been looking for you. Tate's down in the kitchen hunting for some left over cake. Why don't you see if he's saved any for you, all right?"

"Okay," the little girl said, heading around Mo and out the door.

Otis, who hadn't spoken, was left standing alone, with his hands cupped in a deceptively casual way in front of him.

It did little to hide the bulge in his pants.

Mo looked him up and down for a moment, her face giving away nothing but mild curiosity.

"Do you know where my mother is?" she asked.

"Oh, um..." he said, grasping at the possibility that Mo might not realize what had almost been going on in this room. "Uh, she said something about going down to the garden."

"Yeah, okay."

And she left him, breathing an audible sigh of relief.

Mo stood for a moment, watching her mother. Della was lying in the sun on a lounge chair, sporting a bikini that would've bordered indecent on a woman half her age. Large-framed sunglasses obscured her eyes, but there was something about the smile around her mother's mouth that grated on Mo. A combination of smirk and contented cat in the cream.

"Can I ask you something?" Mo said, moving to stand over Della, blocking her sun.

"Oh, honey, can't it wait? It's been such a trying day, and I've finally found a little me time to relax—"

"It's waited for over ten years, Mama. I think it's time."

Della raised her sunglasses and squinted up at her daughter.

"Not this again, love. Can't we let the past be in the past where it belongs? I mean, sure we've all made mistakes. I'm no innocent, and certainly neither are you. Can't we let it lie?" Della said, dropping her glasses back down on her nose and turning her face back to the sky.

"You're blocking the sun, honey," Della said sweetly, with just a hint of irritation.

"One question, and I'll leave you be. Did Roz send you away on the day Lucy was born?"

Mo watched her mother closely. She knew the answer to the question but wondered dispassionately if Della would—if she even could—tell her daughter the truth. Mo didn't miss the split-second of confusion on Della's face before she nodded.

"She did. Of course she did. I wanted to be there for you, Mimosa, but she wouldn't let me be."

Mo examined the woman in front of her. For the first time in her life, Mo realized perhaps it had been a blessing that Della hadn't been a part of her life for the last decade. She'd never go so far as to agree with Roz's methods, but maybe, just maybe, her aunt had done her a favor after all.

Mo felt something settle around her memory of Rosalind Mabry. It wasn't forgiveness. But it was probably the closest thing she'd ever manage. A dawning understanding.

"Mama," Mo said, never raising her voice. "I want you out."

"Excuse me?" Della lifted her sunglasses again, looking at Mo with wide, shocked eyes.

"You and your boyfriend. Out of this house."

"Mimosa, I don't think you understand. I have as much right to be here as you do. More, even. In spite of any names on any pieces of paper, this is my family home."

"Not anymore. You have half an hour. So I suggest you get a move on."

Mo turned to leave.

Della put her sunglasses back on her face and huffed back on the lounge chair.

"That's ridiculous. Now that my sister's dead, I'm here to stay, Mimosa, and you're going to have to deal with that."

"Half an hour, Mama," Mo threw back over her shoulder as she walked away.

Mo found Tate and Sadie in the kitchen. She was glad to see there was some cake left to be had after all. She smiled at their empty plates smeared with chocolate and ran a finger along Tate's and brought it to her lips to taste the little bit of icing left there.

"Guys, I need you to do something for me."

They looked at her in complete trust.

"You go get some bags and pack up anything at all that's precious to you. And I mean anything."

Tate's face clouded with anxiety. He looked at Sadie, then back to Mo.

"Are you dropping us off somewhere?"

She knelt down beside the table and looked them both in the eyes, her face swinging from one to the other.

"Remember, I told you, you're stuck with me now. Got that?"

She waited until they both nodded, then rose.

"Are we moving?" Sadie asked, rising from the table to do as Mo had requested.

"Well," Mo said, "somebody is. Quick now, fast as you can. Get your things and take them over to Calvin's place."

Mo moved to her own room and grabbed her bag from the hook on the back of the door. She stuffed the two manila envelopes into the side pocket.

She walked through the house and out the door, then deposited her bag in the seat of her jeep.

Then she headed for the little shed where the lawn mower and the garden equipment were kept.

Once she'd found what she was looking for, Mo opened the passenger side of her jeep and took a seat sideways with the door hanging open and checked her watch.

Tate and Sadie moved quickly, like she'd asked. She smiled and waved as they took a few duffel bags and other things over to Cal's.

"You get it all?" she asked them.

They nodded. Mo checked her watch again.

"Okay, I've got some things to take care of," she called. "You guys be sure and stay with Cal and Georgia for a while. It's about to get a little messy over here."

"Okay," Sadie called and ran over to Cal's without a second glance.

"Hey, Tate," Mo said, then tilted her head for him to come in her direction.

"I'm serious. Keep Sadie with you, and you both stay with Cal and Georgia. Okay?"

"How long will you be?" he asked.

"Not long at all. Do you trust me?"

"I guess," he shrugged.

She smiled. High praise indeed.

"Okay, go on then," she said.

She watched as Georgia opened the door for him. She could see Cal and Sadie through the big glass windows that Cal had never bothered to cover.

Checking her watch again, she settled in to wait.

Not much longer now.

Mo started in the master bedroom that Della and Otis shared, tipping the red plastic container she'd found in the shed and spilling out its noxious contents.

Otis stood there dumbfounded.

"What... what are you doing?"

"I'm cleaning house," Mo said, moving past him.

"Watch your shoes," she added, as the gasoline made a path out the door and settled into a dark, wet line out into the hallway.

"Della!" Otis yelled.

When some splashed up on his pants leg, he took off running for the front door.

He can move plenty fast for a fat man, Mo thought, then turned back to the task at hand.

By the time Della rushed in the front door, looking as weathered as the old house around her, in her bikini made for a younger woman, Mo had made her way to the living room, emptying the contents of the red can as she went.

"Mimosa Jane! What? Wh..." Della sputtered, her face and eyes wide.

"I suggest you back up, Mama." Mo threw the red plastic gas can into the center of the room.

She ignored her mother's gasp of outrage and wiped her hands together, surveying the room.

Della watched her with her mouth hanging open as Mo walked past her, heading for the table by the open front door.

When she got there, she reached into the basket that had always been where everyone tossed their keys upon arrival and plucked a set she believed belonged to Della.

"Your half hour is up." Mo tossed the keys in her mother's direction.

Della fumbled them, and they fell with a clatter.

"I'd pick those up, if I were you."

Mo reached down and picked up a box she'd placed on the table earlier. It was a small rectangle box of kitchen matches.

Della dropped to the ground, frantically grabbing at the keys, then pushing past her daughter on her way into the sunlight waiting on the other side of the door.

Mo dug one of the red-tipped matches out of the box.

With a flick of her hand, she listened to the satisfying scratch and hiss as the match ground against the side of the box, then caught.

Without hesitation or regret, Mo tossed the lit match onto the floor.

Then she turned and walked out of the old red house as the whoosh of flames took hold.

They all gathered, watching from the yard as Red Poppy Ridge burned. Della was screaming hysterically as Otis tried his damnedest get her stuffed into the passenger side of their car.

"You're crazy! You're a crazy little bitch!"

Mo said nothing, as Otis tried for a second time to get the door closed on his better half.

Finally, he gave the door a determined shove that pushed Della into the seat. He ran around to the driver's side while Della hung half out of the car, yelling obscenities in her daughter's direction.

When Otis put his foot on the gas, he very nearly threw his bikini clad girlfriend out onto the ground, but he didn't slow down and neither did Della's mouth.

When the car disappeared up the road, Mo watched it go, fairly certain that would be the last she ever saw of Della Mabry.

She turned her attention back to the house. Flames could be seen through the windows and smoke was pouring out of the front door and the top of the house.

From somewhere inside there came a crash.

The five of them stood there, the kids' eyes wide with shock and awe.

"You don't do anything by halves, do you Mo?"

"I warned her first," Mo said with a shrug. "I'm a lot of things Cal. Most of them not very admirable. But I'm not a liar."

Cal's place was far enough away not to be in any danger. So they stood there under the east Texas sun and watched it burn. An effigy to a woman Mo had hated, but in the most circuitous of ways, a woman she'd come to almost understand.

Treat it with respect, if you can manage it, Roz had said. Mo doubted a fiery death qualified, but she'd like to think her aunt would understand.

"Hayes is coming," Georgia said.

Mo turned and saw his sedan pulling slowly up the drive.

When he stepped out of the car, he placed his straw fedora carefully on his head, then walked up to the little group.

"Dare I ask?" Hayes said.

Calvin shook his head.

"Call it a controlled burn," he said.

Hayes only sighed.

"Cal, could you keep an eye on these kids. Mimosa, I'd like you to take a walk with me. I planned to do this on the front porch, with a glass of sweet tea, but I suppose the river will have to do."

"What's this about Hayes?" Mo asked.

"I believe you're owed some explanations," said the lawyer.

Calvin looked at Hayes curiously, then nodded, and he and Georgia ushered the kids toward his house.

Hayes held out his arm for Mo to take, a southern gentleman to his core.

The flames were licking up the side of the house as they turned toward the riverbank.

"And somebody call the damn fire department, will you?" he called over his shoulder.

After stopping at his car to retrieve a file box, Hayes and Mo walked to the place she'd come to think of as hers on the banks of the river. It was a presumptuous notion, she knew.

The river had no cares about the concerns—petty or otherwise—of the people who lived and moved around it. To the ancient waterway, they were all ants, crawling this way and that for the briefest blink of time. They came and they went, and the river belonged to none of them, even those whose hearts pulled them back here time and time again.

Hayes set the file box on the ground with a thump.

Mo watched the river and let him say what he needed to say.

"There's plenty of money in the bank," he began, using his handkerchief to wipe the damp from his brow. "Mabry's Soap and Lotion was originally just a way to launder the money Calvin brought in selling marijuana. I don't know if you knew that."

Mo shook her head. She hadn't. She and her aunt rarely talked and never about the ins and outs of her business.

"It did well, almost from the beginning. And over the years, it's only grown. The garden she has here isn't actually where she sells from anymore, except for the occasional limited edition line that might strike her fancy."

Mo wondered if Hayes was aware he still spoke of Roz in the present tense.

"She has a warehouse on the other side of town, run by a manager with a small staff, where the orders are processed, manufactured and sold. So there's that."

Mo tossed a pebble in the river. Except for the small splash, the river was indifferent, flowing onward and away.

"I assume that business up at the house was no accident."

"Hardly," Mo said.

"I thought I told you to stay out of trouble."

Mo shrugged.

"Couldn't be helped."

Hayes sighed again. She was beginning to think of that sigh as his signature. That brought a small smile to her face, and she tossed another pebble.

"That's gonna make things tricky with the permanent custody hearing, Mimosa. Although no one seems to be having any luck finding the girl's mother."

That was a bit of good news.

"Just don't spread it around. Let people think it was an accident, but for God's sake, don't file an insurance claim. I swear I'm running out of favors to spend on you."

Hayes paused. Mo could see he was trying to gather his thoughts.

"Did you know that Rosalind Mabry was the love of my life?" he asked finally.

Mo thought maybe she had.

"If things had been different..." he trailed off, then sent a stern look her way.

"She was, without a doubt, the most difficult human being I've ever had the misfortune to meet. I see a great deal of her in you."

Mo didn't know that she cared for the comparison.

"Damn the woman, sometimes—not often maybe, but sometimes—she was plain wrong."

Mo waited for him to say more.

"You may not believe this, but she loved you. As truly and completely as a mother should. Maybe not as softly, but Mimosa, not all love is soft. When Della came back and took you, you were nearly three years old. Something, something important, died inside of her then. She didn't want that for you."

Mo turned back and tossed another rock. She didn't see any point in arguing with Hayes' view of Roz. It'd serve no purpose at all.

"When Lucy was born and she wasn't breathing, you went mad. Iona sedated you."

Mo's back straightened at the sound of her daughter's name.

"I know that Hayes. I was there."

"What you don't know is that Roz had already planned to try and convince you, by hook or by crook, to give the baby up for adoption. She'd had me working on it for months. She'd chosen the adoptive parents carefully, and they were waiting in the wings. But then the baby was stillborn."

Hayes hesitated.

"Do you know anything about Iona, about how those two came to be friends? Why she had such an undying loyalty to your aunt?"

Thrown by the sudden change in subject, Mo shook her head. She'd never bothered to ask.

Hayes took off his hat and ran a hand through his shocking thicket of white hair.

"I suppose it doesn't really matter. A story for another time, perhaps."

"Why are you telling me this, Hayes?" Mo asked, becoming frustrated with this man who was having such a hard time getting to the point.

"I've come to terms with the fact that Roz used my dead baby as bait to get me back here. I don't like it. And I can't forgive her for it. But honestly, I think—no I know—that nothing else would have worked."

Hayes nodded sadly and placed his hands in his pockets.

"She knew that too. She also knew, from the way you reacted at Lucy's birth, that there was nothing on God's green earth that would have convinced you to give that baby up for adoption."

"She was right."

Mo turned back to the river, hefting the weight of another stone in her hand, so she didn't see his face when he next spoke.

"Which is why, when the baby started to cry, after they'd already given her up for dead, Roz had a terrible decision to make."

Mo had been sitting by the river for what felt like a lifetime. Hayes had left her alone with the file box he'd brought along.

It was full of reports and photographs taken by a private investigator that Roz had kept on retainer for the sole purpose of keeping tabs on her great-niece.

Twelve years old. Lucy was twelve. And eight, and six, and three.

She was healthy. She had her mother's red hair and freckles, Red Beechum's blue, blue eyes.

To anyone else she'd have looked like an ordinary kid. To Mo, she was the most heartbreakingly beautiful thing she'd ever seen. A flesh and blood angel.

Mo stared, she flipped through the photos, and she stared some more.

Her name wasn't Lucy anymore, of course. It was Lila Jane. Lila Jane Kincaid, daughter of Mallory and Stephen Kincaid. And she was living an apparently happy, ordinary middle class life half a state away.

Without her.

"The adoption isn't legal," Hayes had told her. "Your signature was obviously forged. Lucy was essentially kidnapped and given away. Of course, the Kincaids don't realize that. As far as they know, everything was above board."

Mo could only stare at him, feeling untethered from reality.

"Look, I know you need time to process this. But once you do, you've got to realize that a lot of lives hang on a very thin thread that you hold by both ends. My own, for one. If you choose to, you could have me disbarred, at the very least, and potentially thrown in jail. And I won't fight you on it. I'll even recommend a lawyer to represent you for the custody battle."

"Why would you do that?" Mo whispered.

Hayes sighed that signature sigh.

"Because, Mo, in a life led on the shady side of the law, letting her take that baby from you was the single worst thing I've ever done to another human being. Roz assumed I'd keep her secrets after she was gone, because I'm implicating myself by telling you the truth."

Hayes shook his head.

"The woman knew me for nearly sixty years, Mo, and she never understood me at all."

Mo caught a glimpse of just how angry this man was with Rosalind Mabry.

"I'm not gonna stand here and tell you what you should do. It's in your hands now."

Mo didn't know how long she'd been sitting there since Hayes had left her. She'd stared at the images of her daughter until they were branded on her eyes like they'd been forged from the light of the sun.

It was getting dark when she wiped the tears from her eyes.

The last time she'd cried, she'd been numb, abandoned and alone on a stained mattress in a trailer that was left as empty as a papery cicada shell where a tiny heart had once beaten.

This time was different. She cried, not because she was empty, but because she couldn't hold it all in. She had too much inside. The whole world was there. The anger, the grief, the overwhelming joy—and something else. Something she'd forgotten she'd ever known.

It was hope.

With a final swipe at her eyes, she took one of the photos, the one that her eye kept coming back to, of Lila Jane grinning at the camera, one of her front teeth missing and a dirt smudge on her cheek. Then, with all the will in her body, Mo gently placed the photo on the top of the stack and put the lid on the box.

She stood and kicked off her shoes. It seemed like years ago, she'd slid them on, after returning home from a funeral. But she didn't need them now.

Mo waded into the river as deep as she dared, feeling the undertow pull at her ankles and calves while she hugged the box to her chest.

She wondered briefly if she was making the worst mistake of her life.

But she knew she wasn't.

She tipped the box, letting the lid and the contents spill into the river.

And away washed the images of a little girl who had shaped, changed and defined her life in a million different ways.

Mo tossed the box after them, watching as it all floated downstream.

Mo walked back to Calvin's place. Fire trucks had been and gone at Red Poppy. The fire department had made sure the fire hadn't been able to spread and done what they could for the house, but that was little. The big house that had been painted red to strip away any false pretension was stripped of everything now, eaten away by flames and leaving a hulking burned out shell.

Mo tried to pinpoint the emotions that held her now. Surprisingly, given all she'd lost and found and lost again, she felt lighter, somehow. Like great dragging boulders had been unchained from around her neck.

She saw Wade. He'd been speaking to Cal before he stepped into his cruiser. They waved at one another as he drove away.

Calvin had surely filled him in and Wade had wisely decided that tomorrow would be soon enough for any official questions for Mo.

Cal met up with her in front of his house and slung an arm around her shoulder.

She and her uncle walked into his house together.

Tate looked up from his video game, and Sadie ran to her when she came in.

"Where were you?" she asked. "We missed you."

Mo's heart caught in her throat at the simplicity of the love of a child.

Sadie gave her a quick hug, then ran back to the game with Tate. The boy looked at Mo with a question in his eyes, but he settled back when she sent a reassuring smile in his direction.

"I'll get out of your hair," Hayes said, rising from the bar in the kitchen where he'd been speaking with Georgia. "I just wanted to make sure you came back in one piece."

He looked her over worriedly.

"I did. For possibly the first time in my broken life, I'm in one big mended piece."

The lawyer looked relieved.

"Thank you, Hayes," she said.

His eyes widened. Over the years he'd learned never to take anything for granted when it came to the Mabrys, but the last thing he'd expected was her thanks.

"It's done," she said, looking him in the eye. "Over. She's happy where she is. She's loved. And I intend to let it be."

He searched her eyes, then nodded at the conviction there.

He opened his mouth to say something, then shut it again, swallowing the lump in his throat.

After Hayes was gone, Calvin gave her a hug.

He leaned back, his hands on her forearms to look her in the eye.

"I'm sorry, Mo. I didn't know."

She looked at his face, at the sorrow and regret there, and she believed him.

"It's done now. Water under the bridge."

In her mind's eye, Mo saw an image of the sun glinting off of a red haired girl's photo as it sinks below the water.

"Look, Mo," Sadie said. "My painting! Georgia and Calvin let me put it on the mantle."

The girl pointed to the painting Roz had left her in her will.

"I'm glad you remembered to get it, Sadie," Mo said, smiling down at the child's shiny face.

"You said our most precious things."

"I was glad to see you got it also," Calvin added.

"Why's that?" Mo asked.

"Well, Roz has had it for decades, and it was pretty pricey when she bought it. These days, well... I can't even begin to imagine what it must be worth."

Mo took a closer look at the painting of the red Chinese poppies.

The style looked vaguely familiar.

Then her eyes landed on the signature.

"No," she said, her eyes wide, as she turned back to her uncle.

He raised his eyebrows, then nodded.

"This is... this is unbelievable."

"Not really," Cal said. "She had to do something with the bank heist money. She couldn't exactly deposit it in the bank. This took care of about half."

"Ha—Half?" Mo sputtered.

Calvin nodded wryly at his niece's amazement.

"The rest is in bonds in a lockbox welded to the bottom of Tate's old truck."

Mimosa's mouth was still hanging open when Calvin

laughed and clapped her on the shoulder.

"Sadie, did Roz ever tell you about the time she lived out in New Mexico and met a really interesting, talented lady named Georgia?"

"Like Aunt Georgia?"

"Yep," Cal nodded. "Just like that."

Sadie shook her head.

"I'll have to tell you about it sometime."

"But Arlo—She told him, over and over again, it was gone."

Calvin shook his head at her, a kid who'd never learn.

"My big sister was a lot of things, Mimosa. I can't say I ever met a woman with a bigger, more brittle heart. But Arlo was right. She always was a liar."

THE END

A NOTE FROM THE AUTHOR:

Thank you for traveling down this road with me. It was a bumpy ride, to say the least, but I'm so glad you came along. If you'd like, you can follow me on Goodreads, Bookbub or Facebook for updates on my latest projects, or you can find updates at elizamaxwell.wordpress.com. And I can always be reached at theelizamaxwell@gmail.com. Drop me a line. We'll chat.

Also, the powers that be tell me I should use this space to beg, borrow or steal a little more of your time to leave a review. That feels a bit like asking for gifts at a party. Reviews, good and bad alike, are truly appreciated, but my fondest wish is that you had a good time at the party and might be willing to join me again at the next.

It's true that there was a POW camp in east Texas that housed German prisoners of war during World War II, just a few miles up the road from the place where Mexican survivors of the battle of San Jacinto were imprisoned many, many years before that. The site is, in fact, now used as a fairground.

I've taken liberties with those facts, to be used in a fictional sense, but by all accounts, the prisoners were in fact treated kindly and with respect by the residents of Liberty county, according to Miriam Partlow in her book on Liberty County history.

All the best,
~E

ABOUT THE AUTHOR

Eliza Maxwell lives in Texas with her ever-patient husband and two amazing kids. She's a painter, a writer, an introvert, and a British television addict.
In addition, she shares her little corner of the world with a bird named Sarah and a bird dog who lives a tortured existence because of it.

She loves to hear from readers, and you can reach her at mailto:theelizamaxwell@gmail.com.

Made in the USA
Lexington, KY
25 May 2019